PANCHATANTRA STORIES

Sreelata Menon

Illustrations by
Megha Punater

HarperCollins*Children's Books*

First published as 'A Basketful of Animal Tales' in 2019 by
HarperCollins *Children's Books*
This edition published in India in 2024 by
HarperCollins *Children's Books*

An imprint of HarperCollins *Publishers*
Building no 10, Tower A, 4th floor, DLF Cyber City,
Phase II, Gurugram, Haryana - 122002
www.harpercollins.co.in

2 4 6 8 10 9 7 5 3 1

Text © Sreelata Menon 2024
Illustrations © HarperCollins *Publishers* India 2024

P-ISBN: 978-93-6213-058-7
E-ISBN: 978-93-6213-176-8

Typeset in 11.5/19 Century at
Manipal Digital Systems, Manipal

Printed and bound at
Thomson Press (India) Ltd

'All worldly wisdom's inner meaning,
In these five books, the charm compresses
Of all such books the world possesses'
—Arthur Ryder
(Translator)

Contents

What is the Panchatantra?

'Vishnu Sharma!' thundered King Amar Shakti in his most commanding voice, 'My council of ministers tells me you are a great, learned man. If you can't do this, nobody can. If you help me, I will give you more wealth than you can imagine.'

Pandit Vishnu Sharma, who had been summoned before the king, was puzzled. 'Why, your highness, what is the matter? You are king of this ancient kingdom of Mahilaropya. You have everything in the world. What is it you want from me? I am old. I have no great want for wealth or riches. If my knowledge and learning can be of help to you, they are yours for free.'

'After my time, Mahilaropya will need a strong and able ruler,' the king explained. 'Alas, my three sons—Bahu Shakti, Ugra Shakti and Anantha Shakti—are good-natured but dim-witted, disinterested and lazy. Can you teach them how to judge right from wrong and good from bad so that they can become worthy rulers of our great and prosperous kingdom?'

'May I meet with them, your highness?' asked the Pandit, already immersed in deep thought.

So the king called for his three sons to come and meet the learned man. Vishnu Sharma spoke to them for a while and then turned to the worried King, saying, 'Your highness, since they want for nothing and have nothing to do, your sons are just bored. Give me six months, and I will teach them how to live wisely. They will make you proud.'

The king agreed, and his sons were sent off to the Pandit's ashram. Now, Vishnu Sharma knew he needed to develop a strategy interesting enough to engage their minds and keep their attention. So what do you think he did? He invented stories! Tales that involved strong but dull-witted lions, cunning jackals, stupid crocodiles, wily monkeys, lumbering elephants and clever mice. He threw in some fables of turtles, birds, fish, some frogs and even a few owls and crows. It was an ingenious study plan. The stories taught them through example the various rules of 'niti shastra' or principles of governance – in other words, how to rule and live wisely.

Each animal's behaviour and actions highlighted its virtues and vices. This was done in a way that the princes could understand how to bring the messages of the stories into their daily lives. Many stories stressed the need to have and keep intelligent friends. If one story was about how to make friends, another was about how not to lose them. If one was about how to avoid conflict between groups, another was about not losing what one has gained.

In fact, every single story had a message or two. In a charming and witty manner, they also differentiated good from bad and right from wrong. The tales highlighted the qualities that you and I can relate to even today, so many centuries later.

Written in Sanskrit—probably sometime around 200 BC—they were eventually grouped together into five books. Through the years, they became phenomenally popular for their beauty of verse, wisdom and wit. They came to be known as the 'pancha' (five) 'tantra' (practices) because they dealt with:

Losing friends ('mitra bhedha')

Gaining friends ('mitra laabha')

Causing discord between friends ('suhrud bheda')

Losing what was gained ('labdhapranash')

Acting hastily ('aparikshita karakam')

At the end of the six months, the king was a happy man. His sons had turned wise and worthy of being good rulers. Pandit Vishnu Sharma was also content. It was, after all, a job well done!

Shall we now make ourselves similarly wise by delving into this animal kingdom to find out what these stories are all about?

1

The Monkey and the Crocodile

On the banks of a mighty river, there lived a happy little monkey. He lived on a tree that had the most delicious berries in the kingdom. Gorging on them merrily day in and day out, he grew plump and content. He had not a care in the world until the day he had an unexpected visitor – a crocodile.

The crocodile had come out of the river to rest at the foot of the tree. Spotting the monkey, he said, 'I have not eaten in a long time. May I have some berries too?'

'Sure,' said the monkey. 'I'll shake this branch, and you can eat the berries that rain down upon you. How does that sound?'

'Perfect,' said the crocodile, and as the berries fell, he opened his huge big mouth and swallowed them whole in gulps. When he was full, he thanked the monkey and slithered away to the other side of the river, where he lived with his wife. However, he was back the next day and the day after that and, thereafter, every day.

The monkey and the crocodile soon became great friends and would chat for hours as they shared the berries, as good friends do. One day, the crocodile asked for some extra shakes of the berries for his wife. 'I want her to taste these sweet berries too,' he said. The generous monkey obliged, and from that day on, the crocodile always went home with a whole clutch of tasty berries for his wife to enjoy.

After several days, the crocodile's wife thought to herself, 'The berries are so sweet, and the monkey has been living off them for so long. His heart is sure to be as tasty too – maybe even sweeter and softer.' So she told her husband, 'The monkey's heart will be even tastier than the berries. Next time, bring me his heart.' The crocodile was shocked. 'He is my best friend,' he said. 'He has been feeding us every day. It is wicked to talk about eating his heart, even if it is tasty.'

But the more the wife thought about it, the more she liked the idea. She kept badgering and pestering her husband and even threatened to kill herself if he didn't bring her the monkey's heart to eat. The crocodile loved his wife very much and couldn't bear to see her so unhappy. He eventually gave in.

Now, the only way to get the monkey's heart was to invite him home and kill him on the way. So the next time he went over, the crocodile said to the monkey, 'My wife would like to thank you personally for your generosity. Will you come and meet her?'

'Certainly,' said the monkey, quite unaware of the cruel plot. 'But how do I get there?'

'Climb onto my back, and I will ferry you across,' said the crocodile. So the monkey trustingly jumped on the crocodile's back, and they began their journey. Just as they reached the middle of the river, the crocodile suddenly stopped and began to tread water, scaring the monkey.

'What are you doing!' cried the monkey. 'I will drown.'

Thinking it was safe to tell him the truth now, the crocodile said, 'My wife believes that since you have been living off those delicious berries for so long, your heart will be even sweeter. I don't want to kill you, but what can I do? My wife wants to taste your heart.'

The monkey realized he needed to do something quickly if he wanted to survive. Without panicking and with great presence of mind, the monkey said, 'Oh, my friend, you should have told me this before we left the river bank! I don't always carry my heart around with me. I have left it behind on the tree. If I had known that your wife wanted to eat it, I would have brought it along. Now what is to be done? We will have to go back for it.'

The foolish crocodile believed him. 'All right,' he said and turned around. They returned the way they had come. The moment they got back to the bank, the quick-witted monkey scampered off to the highest branch of the tree, leaving the crocodile in the river below.

'You foolish crocodile! Does anyone leave their heart behind?' asked the monkey when he was safe from the crocodile's reach. 'I thought you were my friend. How could you even think of deceiving me so? Go away. You are no longer welcome here!'

The crocodile realized he had been tricked. Due to his wife's greed and his own foolishness, he had lost both the sweet berries and a true friend.

Presence of mind saves the day.

2

The Mongoose and the Mother

I n a little town lived a man and his wife. The wife was expecting a baby. In the same town lived a female mongoose, who was also expecting her baby. On the very same day that the wife gave birth to a lovely little boy, the female mongoose also delivered a perfect little baby mongoose. But alas, the mother mongoose died. The little baby mongoose was left without a mother.

Now the wife was a very compassionate woman. What do you think she did? Feeling sorry for the motherless baby mongoose, she began to look after him just as she did her own beloved newborn. Her baby and the infant mongoose grew up doing everything together. They ate together and drank together. They slept together and played together. The little mongoose never felt the lack of a mother, and he was equally affectionate towards them.

However, there lurked in the wife's mind a constant fear that despite all the love and affection showered on him, the mongoose was, after all, only an animal. She was worried that he could someday harm her son. Not that he had ever done anything that could hurt any of them – but even so, who can vouch for the true nature of any animal?

'Our little boy is asleep. While I'm gone, please keep an eye on him,' she told her husband when she needed to go and fetch water from the well one morning. She left the baby with him and the little mongoose, hoping to be back soon.

A little while later, however, her husband took off to the market. The mongoose was now left alone with the sleeping child. Sniffing around outside, he suddenly spotted a black snake slithering out of a hole in the garden. It was slowly making its way towards the sleeping child within the house.

Now mongooses and snakes are considered to be natural born enemies. Automatically alert, the little mongoose warily watched the snake. When he saw the cobra spread its hood, all set to strike at the dozing child, the little fellow—no more than a baby himself—bared his teeth and threw himself bravely at the big ugly snake.

After a massive fight, the snake finally lay dead, torn to shreds. The mongoose was exhausted but happy he had saved his baby brother. He waited for the mother to return. When he heard her footsteps, he joyfully bounded out to greet her, the snake's blood still dripping about his mouth.

But the moment she saw the mongoose with blood around his mouth, the mother was certain that he had killed her child. She screamed and threw the heavy pot at him. The poor little mongoose, hit by the massive water pot, died on the spot.

The mother rushed into the house, only to find her child gurgling away happily in his corner. All around him, scattered in pieces, lay the blood-splattered body of a big fat ugly snake. At once, she realized what must have happened and rushed back to see if she could revive the little mongoose. 'Wake up, wake up,' she cried. 'I am sorry. I acted in haste. I thought you had killed my son. How could

I have made such a mistake? I should have known you couldn't have done it. Please forgive me.'

Crying and wailing, she set upon her husband who had just returned. 'See what you made me do?' she cried. 'This wouldn't have happened if you had been here to protect the child. Where did you go?'

'I went to the market to earn some money,' he said rather shamefacedly.

'Was there any need to go make more money when you were supposed to look after the baby?' she cried. 'I have killed the mongoose that saved our son. Now what is to be done? I shouldn't have acted without thinking.'

Sadly, the brave little mongoose, for no fault of his, lay dead as a doornail.

Don't jump to hasty conclusions.

3

The Dog Who Left Home

'Woof woof,' barked the spotted dog piteously. Thin and scrawny, he was hungry and looking for food. 'Will I find something to eat today?' he wondered. He scrounged about in dustbins, begged at doors and even tried to steal some leftovers, but there was no food to be had anywhere.

You see, there was a great famine in the country, and food was scarce. Even the people had nothing to eat. Everyone— man, woman, child and animal, including the spotted dog— was trying to survive as best as they could on whatever they could find. Which, if truth be told, was next to nothing.

'If I don't find something to eat soon, I will die. I need to do something quickly,' thought the starving dog. In sheer desperation, he decided to go exploring. He wandered far and wide, foraging for food, till he reached what he believed was another country. This one seemed to be full of delicious fare to eat. He scouted around and found a house whose mistress threw away scrumptious leftovers every day. The spotted dog made himself comfortable there and began to eat up all the waste that was thrown out. Now he had more food than he knew what to do with. He grew fat, and his fur became shiny.

But he forgot one thing – that dogs always mark their territory. They don't like outsiders.

One fine morning, when the spotted dog was still basking in his good fortune, a local dog noticed him. Barking aggressively and growling menacingly at the spotted dog, he began to question him. 'Where have you come from? You look different. You don't belong here. Why are you eating our food?' Soon, other dogs joined him. They surrounded the spotted dog and got ready to attack him.

The spotted dog didn't know what do. He tried to reason with them at first. 'Why do you fear? There is plenty for everyone to eat,' he said. But, in no mood to listen, the local dogs snarled, 'You are not from here. You are an outsider!'

After that, every time he tried to eat, the spotted dog was always viciously attacked by packs of dogs. He soon had to fight for every scrap of food. Scratched and bitten, he began to hurt all over. Even though there was enough food for them all, the other dogs constantly told him, 'This is our land. Go back to where you came from.'

Things came to such a head that, one day, he decided that he had had enough. Even if I stay here forever, they will never accept me as one of their own. I look different, and I come from a different place. They see me as an interloper. They will never leave me in peace. It's not worth it,' he thought.

So he decided it was best to go back.

Back home, to his joy, he was given a hero's welcome. 'Where did you go? You look so good. Are you going back? Will you take us? Is there food for all of us?' the other dogs asked, wagging their tails and licking him all over to show him how happy they were to see him.

'Yes,' said the dog, 'there is food for all of us and more. I was in a wealthy country with nice people. Sadly, however, the dogs there don't like to share, and they attack you constantly because you are different. I tried to fit in, but the local dogs drove me away.' Sighing deeply, he continued, 'It's better to starve with your own kind and live peacefully than be bitten and clawed in a strange land just because they feel you don't belong there – even if it has plenty of everything. That's why I came back.'

Then the spotted dog settled down to sleep. For the first time in many months, he slept peacefully. He slept without any fear of being bitten or threatened. For he was home at last.

Be happy with what you have.

4

The Monkey and the King

A monkey and a king were great friends. The king was extremely fond of him, and the monkey was equally devoted to the king. The monkey lived in the palace and did as he pleased. He ate whatever he wanted, whenever he wanted, and came and went at will – much to the dismay of the royal household. While the king considered the monkey a great companion, all said and done, to the royal staff, he was just a monkey. An animal that needed to be kept in its place.

The king loved to take walks around his kingdom. And it was indeed a beautiful kingdom. With many flowering parks and lovely fountains, it bloomed with colour and was filled with happy chirping birds throughout the year. His faithful companion on these walks was always the monkey, who usually accompanied him uncomplainingly.

On one of their strolls in the garden, the monkey suddenly spotted a snake, poised and ready to strike. 'Your highness,' the monkey said, hopping up and down to attract his attention. 'A snake! Please be careful.' The king saw it and stepped back quickly as the guards rushed to kill the snake.

Pleased with the monkey's alertness, the king thought to himself, 'He is such a loyal and alert fellow. I am sure he will make a good bodyguard.' So he told his courtiers and council of ministers, 'The monkey always looks out for me. I want him as my personal bodyguard.'

'No, no,' said his courtiers. 'How can a monkey be a bodyguard?'

'That's impossible,' cried his worried ministers, 'he is just a monkey.'

'Please, your majesty,' they said with some uneasiness, 'an animal is, after all, only an animal. It does not have the wisdom and the ability of a human bodyguard. Please reconsider your decision.'

But the king was adamant. 'His loyalty cannot be doubted. See how alert he is,' he stated. 'He spotted the snake even before my guards did. I will have him as my bodyguard.' The king did not waver in his decision, and the monkey became his bodyguard – much to the consternation of all his ministers.

One hot summer day, the king decided he needed to rest. He told the faithful monkey, 'I am very tired. Don't let anybody or anything disturb me. I need to sleep.' The monkey, who was as always obedient to the letter, dutifully kept guard while the king went to sleep.

Suddenly, as the monkey kept watch, a fly buzzed in through the window. It buzzed so loudly that he was scared it would awaken the king. He tried to shoo it away with his arms. Then he tried to swing a duster over it. The fly flew this way and that, and every now and then, to the monkey's terrified dismay, it sat on the king. What was most funny was that every time the monkey successfully shooed the fly away, it found a new place to rest on the king's body. Despite the monkey's antics, the fly continued to play catch-me-if-you-can around the king. That is, until it finally decided to settle down comfortably on the sleeping king's neck.

Alarmed, the monkey didn't know what to do. The fly sat unmoving – almost glued to the king's neck. Every ruse to get it off the king without disturbing him had failed, and the monkey was at his wit's end. Desperately, he looked around and spotted the king's sword that was lying beside the king.

Grasping it tightly, he brought it down heavily on the king's neck without a second thought, hoping to smite the fly. Of course, the fly escaped. It promptly flew away. But the sword wounded the king grievously, cleaving his neck in two.

The poor king died, killed by his own trusted bodyguard. The ministers' warnings had come true. Loyal friend though the monkey had been, he turned out to be a foolish bodyguard.

A stupid friend is worse than an enemy.

5

The Goat and the Man

Three friends, who were professional thieves, were hanging about in a village square. They hadn't had a proper meal in days and were hungry. Just as they were wondering what to do, they spotted a man carrying a goat on his shoulders. 'That's a nice fat goat,' said the first thief.

'Yes, indeed. Looks quite juicy too,' agreed the second one. 'Where do you think he is taking it?'

'It will make a fine stew if cooked properly. Shall we try and steal it?' asked the third fellow.

'No,' said the others, 'let's trick the man into giving it to us.' They put their heads together and came up with a foolproof plan to part the goat from the man.

Now, the man with the goat on his shoulder was going home feeling very happy. He had struck a good bargain for the goat. As he hurried along on his way, the first thief accosted him.

'Oh dear sir,' he cried, 'why are you carrying such a filthy dog on your shoulders? It's only fit to be driven away and not carried, surely?'

The man with the goat was taken aback. 'It is not a dog,' he said. 'Can't you see? It is a goat – and a perfectly good one at that.'

'No, sir, it looks like a dirty dog to me! But have it your way,' said the first thief, moving away.

A few miles down the road, the second thief stopped the man with the goat on his shoulders and asked him, 'Sir, why are you carrying this calf on your shoulders? It looks as if it is in need of a wash. Isn't a calf too big to be carried?'

The man with the goat was now doubly shocked. 'First somebody mistakes it for a dog, now this fellow thinks it's a calf. They are mad,' he said to himself. Annoyed, he retorted, 'Are you blind? Can't you see it's a goat? Go away and don't waste my time.'

'No sir, it is a half-starved calf, and why you need to carry it is beyond me. But have it your way,' said the second fellow and moved away.

A few miles on, the third thief crossed the man's path. He asked the man, 'Dear sir, why have you hoisted a donkey on your shoulders? Can't the donkey walk? Who carries a donkey on his shoulders?'

'No, no, no,' said the man with the goat on his shoulders, now exasperated and angry. 'It is a goat, not a donkey. Are the people in this town blind?'

'Well, to me it looks like a donkey, and not a particularly clean one at that. You look silly carrying a donkey around. But have it your way,' said the third chap, moving away.

Now thoroughly confused, the man put the goat down on the road. With a bewildered look on his face, he stared at it and wondered aloud, 'Are my eyes deceiving me? Could these three men be right? How could the goat change from dog to calf to donkey so quickly? It is abnormal.'

He pondered over it for a while. 'Three different men. Surely they cannot all be wrong! It must be a ghost or some supernatural spirit,' he cried in sudden panic. Scared out of his wits at the thought, the silly man let go of the goat and took to his heels in absolute terror.

The three thieves, watching these events from behind a tree, pounced on the goat as it ran past. Hoisting it onto their own shoulders, they laughed at the man's stupidity. They patted themselves on their backs at the success of their plan and set out to cook the mutton stew they were craving. The silly fool who didn't trust his own judgement ran all the way home, cheated out of a great feast.

Use your own judgement and don't blindly believe what others say.

6

The Rabbit and the Lion

'The lion is on the prowl again,' cried the buffalo.

All the animals ran for cover. The lion had a huge appetite, and whenever he felt hungry, he would chase down an animal and make a feast of it. If one day it was a buffalo running for its life, it was a deer or a couple of hares the next day. No animal, big or small, was spared. All of them lived in constant fear. They didn't know who was going to be the cruel lion's next meal, and this uncertainty was taking a toll on them.

The situation got so bad that finally, one day, they got together, hatched a plan and went to meet the lion in his den.

'Why have you come?' growled the surly lion.

'Please, sir, we have come to make you an offer,' said one of the animals. 'Each day, you kill more animals than you really need. From now on, if we send you one animal every day, will you accept it as your dinner and stop killing us as and when you please?'

The lion thought it over and said, 'That's a good idea. I am tired of chasing you around as well. But I have one condition. See that an animal arrives here on time every day. If not, I will start killing again.'

Heaving a sigh of relief, the animals agreed and retreated quickly.

The animals kept their word and sent the lion an animal every day. They took turns to draw lots and then duly sent the unlucky one of their kind to the lion. The rest of them were now free to roam around and graze without fear.

However, all this changed when it was time for the rabbits to send one of their kind to the lion's dinner table. The chosen rabbit was small, but he was a clever little fellow. 'I don't want to die,' he thought, 'but how do I get out of this?'

He made his way slowly towards the lion's den, trying to think of a way to escape. As luck would have it, on the way, he stumbled upon a well. The rabbit saw his reflection in the water, and an idea struck him. He dawdled awhile and then, huffing and puffing, landed up at the lion's den much later than the usual time.

'How dare you come so late?' stormed the lion angrily.

'Sorry, your majesty,' replied the rabbit humbly. 'It is not my fault that I am late. I was on my way here with three other rabbits. Since we are so small, they were meant to be your dinner as well, but we were stopped by another lion. This lion was hungry too. I tried to reason with him, but he wouldn't listen and ate up my three companions. He said *he* was the king of the jungle, not you! He was going to eat me up too, but I managed to escape and somehow reach you.'

'Who is this other lion? How dare he eat up my dinner?' roared our lion. 'Take me to him. Let me see who this imposter is.'

Gleefully, the rabbit took him to the well. 'Look down, your majesty,' he said, 'and you will find him hiding in the well.'

The lion looked down and, indeed, saw a huge ferocious lion staring back at him. So the lion roared. He roared once, he roared twice, and each time his roar of, 'I am the king of the jungle, not you!' came back to him in an echo loud and clear.

'How dare he come to my jungle and tell me I am not king!' said the lion. 'I will teach him a lesson he will never forget!' And so the lion jumped into the well and drowned.

The rabbit quickly scampered home and told all the other animals how he had tricked the foolish lion. The animals applauded the rabbit's cleverness, patting him on the back and thanking him profusely.

Size and strength are no match for a clever mind.

7

The Mice and the Elephants

There was chaos everywhere – trees swayed dangerously, branches broke, stones were overturned, plants were trampled upon. Every time the herd of elephants made their way to the lake, it was as if the earth itself shook.

Unable to get out of the way, scores of little animals lay squeaking and squealing in pain. Hundreds and hundreds of little mice were also usually strewn across the path of the thundering herd. The mouse king held a meeting with all the mice to discuss this problem. 'If this goes on unchecked, we will all be dead before long. We need to do something about it,' said the king. He asked the mice if they had any solutions.

'Why don't you speak to the leader of the elephants and tell them to find another route, your majesty?' suggested one mouse. 'After all, we have been living here amongst the ruins of the village for so long – almost since the day the villagers fled after the earthquake. The elephants may be unaware of the fact that they are trampling through our homes or killing us. We need to tell them.'

'Yes, let's do that,' agreed all the other mice.

A message was sent to the leader of the elephants, and the king of the mice went to meet him. 'You are huge, and we are tiny,' said the mouse king. 'Every time you lead your herd to drink water at the lake, do you realize how many of us you trample upon and kill? We have been living here for years. But if this continues, there will be none of us left alive. Please find another path to the lake.'

The leader of the elephants was good and wise. 'I am sorry,' he said. 'We didn't know we were causing you so much distress. The water in this lake is sweet and fresh. That is why we choose to come here. We will certainly try and find another route.' True to his word, the leader scouted around for another path. All the elephants soon began to go around the ruins to get to the lake, avoiding the homes of the mice.

Years passed. The mice had multiplied in hundreds and were living comfortably amongst the ruins of the village houses when they received a distress call from the elephants. The ruler of the country they lived in had ordered all elephants to be trapped and caught. 'They are strong and intelligent. Let them be trained for work in the kingdom,' he commanded.

Almost all the elephants roaming free were now entrapped, tied up in huge thick nets. However hard they tried, they were unable to get out and were beginning to tire. Could the mice come to their aid? It was the elephant leader's idea to approach them for help.

'Yes,' said the king of the mice. 'You helped us then, and we will help you now. We will have to do it at night, before the king's men come to get you.'

At night, all the mice—every one of them, from the baby mouse to the grandmother mouse—rushed down in their thousands to where the elephants were being held. They soon got to work with their sharp little teeth. Nibbling away at the nets that held the elephants, they made large holes and, one by one, set all the elephants free before daybreak.

The leader of the elephants thanked the mice and gratefully herded all his elephants away to another faraway forest before the trappers could discover their escape or take them away. The mice quickly scampered home as well.

'So what if we are small? Every good deed must be repaid, as we have done,' said the mouse king, rubbing his little hands in satisfaction.

One good deed deserves another.

8

The Camel and the Bell

'Stay with the rest of us,' the older camels advised the young camel. 'Don't wander about in the jungle on your own. The sound of your bell might attract a lion or a tiger on the prowl.' For whenever the young camel moved his head, the bell around his neck jingled and the pleasant sound wafted in the breeze.

However, the young camel was an arrogant little fellow who considered himself superior to other camels and always held himself aloof. He generally grazed away from the herd and often wandered away on his own. 'I am different from the other camels,' said the young camel. 'None of the others have a bell round their neck. So I must be special.' And he was indeed special to his owner, the cart-maker, who was extremely fond of him.

Now the cart-maker had once been dirt poor. Unable to make a living making carts, he had decided to leave home and try his luck in another town. While travelling with his wife and child, he had stumbled upon a female camel trying to deliver her baby all by herself. He had stopped to help her, and once the baby camel was born, the cart-maker and his wife had taken them along to their new abode. There, all of them had flourished.

The cart-maker took to selling camel milk and began to make a lot of money. Since selling camel milk was a more profitable business than cart-making, he asked himself, 'Why don't I start breeding camels as well? I only need to buy more camels. I can not only sell the milk but also the baby camels.'

The cart-maker's camel business took off so well that he was soon able to employ people to help him. The camels were very well looked after. They had plenty of food to eat and enough space to graze in. Although they lived at the edge of a jungle, the cart-maker made sure that they there safe and secure. On the whole, they were a happy lot.

All the same, despite the many camels he now owned, the cart-maker's favourite was always the baby camel he had helped deliver in the jungle, which was why he had tied a bell around the young camel's neck. Whenever the cart-maker heard the bell, it gladdened his heart. Yes, the callow young camel certainly held a special place in the cart-maker's heart.

If only he had listened to his elders.

A lion in the jungle was looking for food when he happened to hear the jingle of the bell. He heard it again the next day and the day after that as well. 'What could it be?' he wondered. He decided to investigate. He followed the sound of the bell and discovered it was our young camel.

'Well well well,' said the lion to himself, 'What a lovely piece of meat. I am sure he will be juicy as well.' But he couldn't do much as the young camel was at the lake in the midst of all the other camels.

The lion now began to keep watch from amongst the bushes. He noticed that the young camel was often on his own, so he lay in wait for a chance to strike. Sadly, once when the young camel was arrogantly grazing by himself as usual, he lost his way. Trying desperately to find his way home, he wandered further into the jungle.

The lion decided that this was his chance. As the camel dithered around, the lion pounced on him and, in a flash, the poor young camel lay dead. If only the young camel had heeded the advice of the older camels and not strayed. He wouldn't have got lost nor would he have been killed.

Pride goes before a fall.

9

The Jackal, the Lion, the Leopard and the Tiger

The jackal circled the elephant once. He circled him twice. He went around him a third time, just to be sure. Yes, the elephant was dead all right. 'I wonder how he died,' thought the jackal. 'Anyway, it doesn't matter. I won't go hungry for the next few days at least.'

He tried to bite into the elephant. But his hide was too thick. He just couldn't get a grip on the flesh. So he began to circle him again, but he still couldn't find a place tender enough to sink his teeth into.

Just then, a large lion came by. 'Hi, jackal, what do you have here?' he asked.

'It is a dead elephant, your majesty. Would you like to take the first bite? After all, you are the king of the jungle,' the jackal said humbly.

'No, no, jackal, I don't eat anything that is not fresh nor what others have killed. You go ahead. But thank you for asking,' replied the lion, going his way.

'Well,' thought the sly jackal, 'that worked out all right. My humble attitude got rid of the lion quickly, or he might have stayed to feast.'

He was still wondering how to get at the elephant meat when in wandered a leopard.

'Oh,' said the jackal to himself, 'here is another fellow that is fond of flesh. Now how do I get rid of him? I will have to be cunning.'

The leopard was hungry. He looked longingly at the carcass.

'Oh dear, what brings you here, Mr Leopard?' asked the jackal. 'This elephant is a lion's kill. The lion is very annoyed with leopards at the moment for poaching his kills. Do you think this carcass is worth a fight with the king of the jungle?'

'No, it isn't worth a fight,' decided the leopard. 'Don't tell him I was here. Thank you for warning me. I will be on my way.'

Relieved, the jackal was busy patting himself on the back at his cleverness when he realized he was still nowhere

closer to dining on the elephant than before. And before
the jackal could make another attempt, who should saunter
in but a tiger! 'I should make use of the tiger's sharp teeth
to cut into the elephant's hide before I get rid of him too,'
he decided.

'A lion has just made this kill,' said the jackal to the tiger,
pointing to the dead elephant. 'He has gone to the river to
clean up and will be back. You look hungry and half-starved.
Why don't you take a few bites of the elephant before he
returns? I will warn you when he is near.'

'Indeed, I am hungry,' said the tiger. 'But I don't want to
annoy the lion. After all, it is his kill.'

The jackal knew if he didn't do something fast, the tiger
would leave. So he called out, 'Don't be a coward, Mr Tiger.
Nothing is gained by running away. Eat your fill. I will warn
you before the lion returns. Come back.'

The tiger was extremely hungry. He didn't hesitate again. He dug into the carcass with his sharp teeth. However, the moment the tiger tore the hide open and pushed out the soft flesh, the jackal warned him, 'He is coming. He is coming. Quick, run!'

The poor tiger, still hungry, simply took to his heels. Our cunning jackal now happily sat back to eat the tender flesh carved out by the tiger.

However, just as the jackal began to eat, another jackal popped up from out of the jungle. He made a beeline for the carcass as well. This annoyed our jackal. Unlike in the case of the lion, the leopard and the tiger, he felt he could take on this fellow and fight him if necessary. After all, it was a jackal just like himself, not a stronger animal.

Snarling and growling, our jackal ferociously attacked the other jackal and chased him away. Proud of his quick wit and happy that his plans had worked, he triumphantly settled down to dine on the poor dead elephant.

Plan your strategy well.

10

The Donkey That Loved to Sing

'Have you finished?' asked the jackal. 'Let's get out now before the farmers come out to see who is amongst their crops.'

'Don't worry,' said his companion confidently. 'When they look out and see the tiger skin on my shoulders, they will think I am a tiger. They will be too scared to come out.'

'But you aren't one. You are only a donkey. Now let's go before we are caught,' said the jackal, leading his friend away.

The donkey belonged to a poor washerman, who had no money to feed him. They both worked hard throughout the day. While the washerman scrubbed, washed and laundered clothes for a pittance, the donkey helped him carry and fetch loads and loads of washed and dirty clothes every day, despite how lean and hungry he was. The washerman was barely able to make ends meet and would himself go to bed hungry on most days.

After each day's hard work, the washerman would drape a tiger skin on the donkey's back and let him wander at night to feed amongst the fields and farms of the neighbourhood. He hoped that the tiger skin would trick the farmers so that they would not investigate. The donkey continued to use his disguise and soon grew fat and plump.

On one such outing, the donkey had stumbled across a jackal, who was also on the same mission. They soon became great friends. While the donkey ate up the barley and the cucumber in the fields, the jackal feasted on the chickens and hens in their coop, and the farmers were none the wiser. They continued to be fooled into thinking it was a tiger. Despite the tiger skin, however, the jackal always worried that they would be found out, so he would try to hurry his friend to finish up before daybreak. But the donkey was not afraid at all.

One night, after a great meal, the donkey wanted to sing. 'Please let me sing,' he told the jackal. 'The night is young, and the moon is bright, and it's a lovely night for some good music.'

'Don't be stupid,' said the jackal. 'You will wake up the farmers. In any case, you have a terrible voice.'

'You just don't appreciate good music,' the donkey argued. 'The ragas, the talas and the scales are exquisite.

Music is divine. Anyway, what do you know of it? You are just a jackal.'

'That may be,' said the jackal, 'but I know foolhardiness when I see it. It is silly to draw attention to ourselves. The moment you start to bray, the farmers will know you are only a donkey and chase us away.'

The donkey was in no mood to listen. Under the bright moonlight, everything looked so beautiful he felt he just had to sing.

'Well, then I am off. I will watch from outside the farm gates. I don't want to get caught,' said the jackal sensibly, and off he went to hide.

The donkey began to sing. 'Hee haw, hee haw,' he sang, unaware of how terrible he actually sounded.

The donkey brayed so loudly that every farmer in the vicinity came out. They soon realized it wasn't a tiger at all but a donkey in a tiger's skin. Angered at being fooled, they beat him up mercilessly with their sticks. 'Take that for stealing our crops,' they said, hitting him over and over again. Then, tying a heavy stone to his neck, they told him, 'Come anywhere near our crops again, and we will kill you,' and drove him out of their fields.

The donkey tottered home, hurting all over. Saddened and much wiser, he told the jackal, 'Dear friend, you were right. I should have listened to you, and I should not have pretended to be something I was not.'

Do not pretend to be what you are not.

11

The Frog and
the Fish

A frog and a couple of fish were in the midst of a heated discussion. 'You heard the fishermen,' said the frog. 'They will be back tomorrow with large fishing nets and baskets to capture us all. We need to get out now.'

'No' said the first fish. 'Just because we overheard something scary, it doesn't mean we are in any real danger.'

'I agree,' said the second fish with the smooth grey skin. 'Nobody leaves home based on a mere suspicion. I may not be as learned as you,' he said to the first fish whose scales shone like polished marble. 'After all, you are known as Sahasra-buddhi, which means you are 1000 per cent

41

brainy. But I am called Shatha-buddhi. That means I am 100 per cent brainy, and I also think we shouldn't run away from our home.'

'If they do come, there are ways to escape the nets,' said the first fish.

'We can dive down deeper or maybe go around the mesh,' agreed the second fish. 'This lake is such a beautiful place to live in. The waters are deep and blue, and all our friends are nearby.'

'I may not be as brainy or learned as both of you,' said the frog. 'That is probably why I am called Eka-buddhi, which means I am only one per cent brainy. But all the same, something tells me that if we don't go now, we are doomed.'

'Don't be such a coward,' mocked both his fish friends in unison. 'We vote to stay.'

The frog hesitated awhile, but then said decisively, 'No. you may mock me and laugh at me, but I vote no. I am not taking any chances.' And so, he bid goodbye to both his friends, bundled up his family of little frogs and hopped across to the banks of the lake. They parked themselves under a rock inside a well where they would be safe.

Meanwhile, his two fish friends continued to swim the waters of the lovely lake where they had lived all their lives. They grumbled to each other, 'We can't run away at the first sign of danger, can we? What use is our intellect and learning if we don't put them to use to save ourselves? If they come tomorrow, we will try and out-swim and out-dive their nets. After all, unlike the frog, *we* are learned and clever.'

The next day dawned bright and sunny. At daybreak, the two fishermen arrived with their paraphernalia. 'Look at all these lovely fish!' said one, dropping his rods and hooks. 'It will be a good catch.'

'Yes, let's not waste time,' said the other, quickly spreading his nets and baskets.

Sahasra-buddhi didn't give in without a fight. He did his level best to escape. He dived deep down, but the net spread even deeper. He tried to break through the nets, but they held even tighter. As for Shatha-buddhi, he didn't stand a chance. The fishermen caught him on the dive and threw him straight into a basket, from which he couldn't escape.

Before long, almost every one of the little creatures swimming in the lake was netted. While some unknowingly fell to the fish hook, others took the bait and scores of fish, frogs, tortoises and crabs were reeled in with no chance of escape. Happy with their tremendous catch, the men set out for their homes. Slung triumphantly across their shoulders was Shatha-buddhi and on their heads was Sahasra-buddhi, the heaviest and largest fish in the lake.

The frog watched these events sadly from under a rock. He croaked mournfully to his wife, 'What use was all that learning to Sahasra-buddhi or Shatha-buddhi? Common sense told us to escape, but alas, they thought they knew better and perished. All the learning in the world is useless if common sense deserts clever people.'

It is better to be safe than sorry.

12

The Cobra and the Ants

The huge black cobra slithered out of his hole. He spread his enormous hood and looked around. His forked tongue darted to and fro rapidly, and his glimmering eyes were anything but kind. The little creatures of the forest knew they were in danger. If they didn't scurry away in time, they would be the cobra's meal of the day.

It was the same every night. The cobra would come out at dusk to hunt for prey. It could be anything – a lizard, a frog, a mouse, a sleeping bird or its eggs. They would be gone in a jiffy, crushed and swallowed whole even before they knew it. No creature escaped the cobra's greedy venomous fangs.

At daybreak, he would slither back into his hole and sleep the day away. And so it continued – night after night. With no one to oppose him, the cobra grew fatter and fatter, while his ego grew even bigger and bigger. After all, he was a King Cobra, wasn't he?

'What do we do?' asked the other little animals of each other. 'He comes upon us so silently that there's no time to escape.'

'Yes,' they agreed sorrowfully, 'his fangs are so poisonous that we don't stand a chance.'

'He has eaten so many of us that he has grown fat!' remarked a squirrel.

'True,' said the mouse, 'very soon he won't be able to fit into his hole.'

As they had predicted, the snake soon grew so huge and fat, he found himself unable to get into his hole. 'I am the king of the forest,' thought the cobra to himself, 'I should be able to make my home anywhere.' He searched high and low for a place to live. Finally, he found a large hole in a tree similar to his old one. He highhandedly told all the animals who lived there, 'I am going to live here from now on, so get out – all of you!'

In any case, even before the cobra had uttered a word, the moment they had seen him, all the little animals living there had already begun to run for their lives. The rabbit hurriedly took away her little bunny family, and little Mrs Mouse did the same with her babies. The birds took their eggs up to nest amongst the higher branches while the lizards and the frogs swiftly slunk away. Only the ants remained in their anthill next to the hole in the tree.

'Escape when you can,' the others advised the ants. 'You know how dangerous he is.'

'Don't worry, he can't do anything to us,' said the ants.

'Oh, can't he?' hissed the big-headed cobra, overhearing them. 'I will teach you a lesson you will never forget.' He then set about destroying the anthill. He threw himself about this way and that till the anthill was reduced to a pile of mud. Many ants lay crushed and dead.

'Told you to get out,' said the other animals as they slipped away.

However, the queen ant called out to all her little workers and said, 'We need to teach this arrogant cobra a lesson once and for all. You know what to do. Now get to work.'

Immediately, thousands and thousands of little ants came scurrying out of every little hole in the ground in the most orderly fashion you can imagine. Before the conceited cobra knew what was happening, they had swarmed all over him. They bit him on his face, his hood, his body and his tail. They didn't leave an inch free. The cobra squirmed and struggled, wriggled and twisted but couldn't escape them. Writhing in pain and stung all over, his ego in tatters, the 'king of the forest' lay almost dead – defeated by the tiniest of tiny creatures of the forest.

'If we work together even the small and the weak can take on the strong and the arrogant,' remarked the owl on the tree, plumping his feathers and nodding his wise old head.

'Yes, indeed. Thank you, dear ants. You've rid us of a bad enemy,' cried all the other little animals in gratitude.

Teamwork pays.

13

The Jackal That Turned Blue

The jackal began to run. He ran and he ran and he ran so fast that he could feel his heart thumping hard against his chest. 'Will it pop out of my mouth?' he wondered. Yet, there was no respite. The dogs kept after him, snarling and growling. They were local dogs and didn't like outsiders. They had begun to chase him when they found him foraging for food in their market. 'Hungry or not, you belong in the jungle. Why have you come here?' they barked.

The jackal was outnumbered and too scared to fight back. He ran into a shed. It was a dyer's shed. And he fell straight into a huge tub of blue liquid. The dogs followed, but the jackal dived deeper into the liquid and kept absolutely still. Only the tip of his nose showed. Unable to find him, the dogs left.

The jackal waited until he was certain the dogs had all gone. Then, wet and cold, he attempted to make his way back to the jungle. Alas, the dogs spotted him. This time, though, they yelped in fright and ran away. They didn't know what to make of him! The blue dye had made him grotesque and unrecognizable. Surprised but relieved, he made his way home.

'What kind of animal is that?' asked the tiger anxiously.

'Is it an animal at all?' wondered the lion.

'Then what is it?' demanded the bear, perplexed.

'Can't you see he is blue?' stated a rather bewildered elephant.

'Definitely not a jackal,' said the jackals, shaking their heads.

'He looks scary,' said the wise old owl when they saw him enter the jungle.

Being a quick-witted fellow, the jackal kept quiet. 'I must look very different,' he told himself. 'They seem to be frightened of me. I can perhaps use it to my advantage. If they don't know I am a jackal, why tell them?'

'Why are you scared?' he called out to the others. 'I won't harm you.'

'You look strange,' they replied nervously. 'We haven't seen you here before. Who are you?'

'God has sent me to be your king,' he announced regally. 'I am King Kukudruma.'

The lion, the tiger, the elephant and all animals of the jungle had been ready to flee only moments ago, but now they stopped to listen.

'I am here to take care of you. I will assign you some duties, and we will all live in peace,' said the jackal.

The animals were taken in by his words. 'We are pleased to have you as king,' they said. 'Tell us what you want, and it shall be done.'

The jackal was smart. He arranged duties for all the animals and began to sort out their problems as and when they cropped up. For himself, he asked only for loyalty and an animal a day for his meals. However, afraid the other jackals might recognize him as one of their own, he made sure to banish all the jackals to the outskirts of the jungle. The animals were completely fooled and didn't grudge him a thing. They looked after his every need and did everything to please him.

Days went by. The blue jackal continued to play king and the animals were none the wiser. Occasionally, he felt homesick for his own kind. But he knew that to have them anywhere near was to invite danger. They could recognize him and reveal his secret, and he would lose his power over the animals. So he continued to keep them away.

However, one day he heard a pack of jackals howling in the distance. Unable to contain his excitement at hearing the cries of his own kind, he involuntarily let out a happy howl in response. This stopped all the animals in their tracks.

'Is he a jackal?' they wondered in shock, recognizing the sound. It suddenly dawned on them that they had been fooled.

'How dare you trick us?' they asked angrily. They felt mortified that they had been fooled by a mere jackal and, in a flash, turned against him. They attacked him ferociously. The poor blue jackal didn't stand a chance. He was unable to save himself. Since he had driven away all the other jackals and had been careful to keep himself aloof from everyone, there were none of his kind to come to his rescue either. Severely outnumbered, the jackal died miserable and alone.

Don't pretend to be what you are not.

14

The Cat, the Hare and the Partridge

The partridge flew around the tree. Round and round she went. She was looking for her home in the tree. 'Could I be wrong?' she asked herself worriedly. 'I am sure this is the same tree I used to live in. Is there someone else in the hollow now?'

Just then, a hare popped out of the hole in the tree and asked her in an irritated voice, 'What is your problem? It's cold and all that flapping about is only making it colder. Don't you have other things to do?'

'This was my home,' said the partridge. 'I used to live here in this hollow for years.'

The hare's long, pointed ears twitched frantically. 'Well it's not your home now,' he said, annoyed at being disturbed. 'It's my home now. Why did you go away?'

'It was summer. There was no food to be had here,' said the partridge. 'But I found plenty of grain amongst the wheat and rice fields in another land. I've been living there.'

'So why have you come back?' asked the hare.

'It's winter. It's cold out in the open,' replied the partridge. 'I've returned to what was my house. I want my home back.'

'Well, you can't have it,' said the hare. 'It was empty. I found it, so now I get to keep it!'

'No, it was my home first,' insisted the partridge, flapping her wings vigorously. 'I want it back.'

'Sorry, you can't have it back. It's mine now,' the hare repeated.

The argument between them raged on for many hours. Neither was willing to give in. Finally, tired, the partridge said, 'Why don't we ask a third person to hear us out and judge as to who is right? We could settle this argument once and for all.'

'Yes, we need someone wise and impartial to decide,' the hare agreed. As they looked around, they spotted an old cat comfortably perched on a tree, licking herself warm. The partridge was a little hesitant. Cats are known to eat birds. She asked the hare, 'Do you think it is safe to ask the cat? She might be dangerous.'

'Why not?' replied the hare. 'She seems to be an old cat. I have heard she is wise and learned. In any case, what can she do to us? If she attacks us, I'll run, and you can fly away.'

They went up to the cat, making sure they stood at a safe distance.

Now the cat was a greedy old killer cat. She was both hungry and cunning and was thrilled to see the two of them. 'If only I can get my paws on them, I will have enough food to last me a long, long time,' she told herself. 'I wish they would come nearer. I need to persuade them to come to me. I think I will pretend to be deaf.'

'What is the matter, dear?' called out the sneaky cat to the hare and partridge.

'Well you see, we have this problem—' started the hare.

'Come nearer so I can hear you properly. I am old. I can't hear or see well,' she yelled back.

The two were a bit uneasy.

'Come closer,' shouted the sly cat again, quite winningly. 'There is nothing to be worried about.'

Reluctantly, they crept nearer. The moment they did, the wicked old cat struck the hare hard with her paws and attacked the partridge with her teeth before they could even react.

'Stupid creatures,' she purred, licking her lips in glee. 'They should have known better than to approach a hungry cat.'

Never ask or trust a third person to settle an argument.

15

The Doves and the Hunter's Net

The hunter watched in amazement. His net was high in the sky. Gently wafting away, it was being carried by scores and scores of lovely grey and white doves. He scratched his head in disbelief. The doves were actually carrying away the trap he had set for them. 'How can this be?' he wondered.

It all began on a summer day when an owl who lived on a huge peepal tree overheard the hunter talking to himself. 'It's been a hard year,' the hunter said. 'Food has been difficult to come by. This tree seems to have a lot of birds. I could perhaps trap some of them in my net.' As the owl watched, the hunter set about laying a trap for the birds. He arranged his net, making sure that it was carefully hidden. He spread some grains far and wide on the ground before leaving, satisfied he had done his best.

The peepal tree was home to a host of beautiful birds. As soon as the hunter had gone, the owl warned all of them, 'A hunter has laid a trap. Don't eat the grains spread under our tree, or you will be caught in his nets. It is best to fly away now.'

Heeding the owl's warning, the other birds quickly flew away without touching the grains. Unfortunately, a dole of doves flew in a few minutes later. They hadn't heard the warning. They had been flying for a long time in search of food and were tired and hungry. The moment they saw the scattered grains, they excitedly swooped down to fill their little bellies. When they landed and started to peck at the grains, the hunter's net dropped down on them. They tried desperately to escape, clawing at the nets with their tiny little feet and biting into it. They pecked and they fluttered against it. They did all they could to tear through it, but to no avail. The net held fast and steady.

Their king, however, was a resourceful bird. 'Don't try to get out individually,' he told the other doves. 'It will be a waste of time and effort. We must work together as a team before the hunter returns. Now each of you take a piece of the net in your beaks. We will lift it all together at the same time and try to fly away to where our friends the mice stay. They will help us.'

The doves followed their king's advice. Slowly, they found themselves rising into the air with the net. He made them fly a few miles, to where the mice lived.

As the doves flew higher and higher, the hunter spotted them. Dismayed, he watched for a while and realized that there was nothing he could do. The doves had outwitted him. Disappointed, he went home. He had lost his grains and his net and had not even managed to catch a single bird.

As soon as the doves reached the mice, the king of the doves asked the mice, 'Will you help us, dear friends? Can you nibble at the net and set us free?'

'Certainly,' said the mice, once they got over the surprise of so many doves landing up at their place with a net. They quickly set about gnawing them loose with their sharp teeth. Soon, the doves were fluttering free in joy.

'Thank you, my friend. You have saved our lives,' said the dove king to the king of the mice.

'Great things can be achieved if we work together,' said the mouse king, nodding.

If the owl hadn't warned the other birds, they might have fallen prey to the hunter. If the doves hadn't worked together, they would have been trapped in the hunter's net. If the mice hadn't worked to free them, they wouldn't have been freed.

Separately, they might have failed. United, they won.

There is strength in unity.

16

The Crab and the Crane

The crane stood alone on a rock by the lake. The fish swam to safety, the frogs hopped away, and all the other water creatures began to hide. Nobody wanted to be the crane's meal of the day. But strangely, the crane wasn't hunting that day. He just stood like a statue and gazed mournfully at the water.

One by one, the animals in the lake began to murmur. 'Why is he not attacking us?' they wondered. Only the crab had the courage to ask him. 'Hey, Mr Crane,' he called, parking himself far away. 'What is the matter? Why are you so sombre and quiet? Why aren't you stalking us?'

Now the crane was both cunning and wicked. He was very old and hungry as well. Finding it difficult to hunt for food, he was growing weaker and weaker. In desperation, he had come up with a plan and had been waiting for just this opportunity. He quickly looked towards the crab and said, 'Haven't you heard the news?'

'No,' said the crab.

'This lake is soon going to dry up and none of us are going to survive,' said the crane. 'So I have decided not to eat any of you. After all, we have lived together in this lake for a long time now.'

Agitated, the crab rushed to tell the others what the crane had said. 'What do we do?' he asked.

'It must be true,' said the fish, 'since he isn't trying to catch us.'

'Ask him what to do,' said the frog, hopping out of his hidey hole.

'There is another pond nearby,' said the crane, as if letting them in on a secret. 'It has plenty of good water. I was planning to go there. I could take you all there if you like.'

'Yes, please take us there,' pleaded all the little animals without a moment's hesitation.

'All right, I will,' said the crane, pretending to be reluctant. 'But I will have to do it one by one. It will take many days.'

'It doesn't matter,' said the crab, 'so long as we are safe.'

All the animals agreed, and there was great rejoicing at the lake that night. The crane was going to save them after all!

The crane began to take them one at a time. He would fly to the other side of the lake with the animals on his back, where he would smash them up and eat them whole before flying back, his hunger satisfied. He would do it all over again the next day. This went on for a long time with none of the animals being any the wiser.

'Who would have thought the crane would save us? They must be happily swimming in the other lake,' thought the other animals.

One day, the crab asked the crane, 'Why don't you save me next?'

'I am a bit sick of fish,' the crane thought to himself. 'Crab meat will be a nice change.'

'Why not?' he replied. The next time he flew out, he took the crab along on his back.

'Where is the lake? Where is the water?' asked the crab when they reached the place where the crane usually ate them up.

The crane replied, 'There is no lake and no water. I am going to eat you up just like I ate the others. See those piles of bones on a rock?'

The crab on the crane's back was nothing if not quick-witted. He realized he had to do something fast if he wanted to stay alive. Without a word, he moved forward and tightened his grip on the crane's throat. The crane desperately tried to shake him off, but the crab simply continued to squeeze and slowly strangled the crane to death. Huffing and puffing, the crab dragged the dead crane back to the lake. 'What have you done?' the other animals cried, 'You have killed our saviour!'

'Saviour, hah!' said the crab, recounting all that had happened. 'We should have checked to see if the news was true before going with him. He was a wicked old cheat who was killing us one by one to satisfy his hunger. We were fooled by him.'

The animals were saddened to hear this. 'We shouldn't have trusted the crane so blindly,' they all agreed.

Never believe anyone blindly.

17

The Cobra and the Farmer

'My son,' said the farmer, 'I need to go out of town for a few days. Do you see the anthill next to that tree there?'

'Yes,' nodded the son.

'A cobra lives there,' stated the farmer. 'Will you give that cobra some milk every day till I return?'

'Yes, father, I will. But why do you give the cobra milk?' asked the son.

'One afternoon long ago, on a hot summer day,' explained the farmer, 'when we were poor and could hardly make ends meet, I saw this cobra come out of that anthill. I sought its blessings by leaving a bowl of milk for it. The next day, I found a gold coin in the bowl. Since then, I have left some milk for it every day, and in return, I always find a gold coin in the bowl. Today, we have enough food to eat and more. Our farms are thriving, and we have a good collection of gold coins saved up for a rainy day. It is all due to the cobra's blessings, so don't forget to give it milk.'

'I won't forget,' said the son, and every day, he dutifully put out a salver of milk for the cobra. Each day, just like his father had said, he found that the milk was all gone and a gold coin left in its place.

Unfortunately, the son was young, impatient and quite greedy. He was tired of having to wait every day for a single gold coin. He thought to himself, 'Hmmm … If the cobra can bring out a gold coin every time he is given milk, he must have lots of gold coins stashed inside the anthill. Why don't I kill the cobra, destroy the anthill and collect the gold coins all at once?'

He decided to act before his father returned. The next day, instead of leaving the milk and going away as usual, he lay in wait for the snake. As the cobra appeared, he brought down a heavy stick on its head. To the son's bad luck, the blow injured the cobra but did not immediately kill it. The cobra was in pain and reacted violently. It lashed round angrily and bit the boy. The boy died on the spot.

The farmer returned a few days later. He was greeted with the sad news of his son's death. He realized his son's greed must have made him attack the cobra. Instead of grieving for his son as everyone expected him to do, he rushed to the anthill with some milk. 'I am so sorry,' he said, 'that my son tried to kill you.'

'What are you doing here?' asked the snake in annoyance. 'Your son is dead, and you have come to see me instead of mourning him. Are you hoping for more gold coins?'

'I am sad that my son is dead,' replied the farmer, 'but he shouldn't have attacked you.'

The cobra was in no mood to listen. 'Is there no limit to your greed?' he asked angrily. 'Your son was greedy too. That's why he did what he did. He was young and ignorant, and for his greed, he paid with his life. And instead of weeping over your dead son, you are here to collect more gold! Has your greed made you blind to everything? Do you love gold even more than your son? I don't trust you anymore. Don't come here again.'

'But … please,' stammered the farmer.

'No,' continued the furious cobra. 'I don't want to hear anything. Take this diamond as a last and final gift from me and don't come here ever again.' The snake swished around and disappeared into the anthill forever.

The farmer rued his son's greed. Through no fault of his own, he had lost not only his son but also the cobra's trust and his supply of gold coins.

Trust once broken cannot be mended.

18

The Monkey and the Piece of Wood

There lived a group of playful monkeys in a jungle. Day in and day out, they hopped from tree to tree and swung happily on big vines. They grabbed at berries. They tugged at twigs. They broke off bunches and bunches of huge bananas. They ate them and stamped on them, squashed them and even chucked them at each other. Chattering and screeching as monkeys generally do, they were always at play. If it was not hide-and-seek, it was catch-me-if-you-can, and when they got bored of this, they simply chased each other around.

Once, their daily games brought them to the edge of the jungle, where they chanced upon a group of men working on a building. Now these men were building a temple. Their work was still half-finished, so they laboured hard throughout the day and usually only took a break for lunch. The monkeys had landed up there shortly after the workers had put down their tools and gone for their break. The monkeys were intrigued by the building. They decided to play around the half-finished temple.

Curious, they began to explore the temple, and a flurry of conversations started:

'What do you think this is?'

'It is a building. Look, it's got windows and doors. It looks like they are going to put a roof over it too.'

'Where are the men?'

'They must have gone to have lunch.'

'Let's have some fun before they come back.'

One of the monkeys started to swing from one wooden beam to another. Very soon, all the monkeys followed suit. They jumped through half-open doorways, swung from one lintel to the other and played hide-and-seek behind the planks. While some monkeys threw the workers' tools at each other, others loped around the entire structure and toppled whatever they could topple. Up and down and up and down they went, trying out every pillar and column.

While all the monkeys were thus busy, one little monkey was more curious than the others. She spotted a piece of wood sticking out halfway between two half-sawn pieces of a log.

'What is that?' asked the inquisitive little monkey.

'Don't meddle with it,' warned the others. 'You will get hurt.'

The carpenters had been slicing a log into two. To keep the two halves separate, they had driven a small wedge of wood between the two pieces. Our little monkey did not know that. And she wasn't about to listen to the others' advice either. She sat with her tail in between the open halves of the log and tugged and tugged at the wedged piece that was keeping the two halves separate.

'Be careful, you might get stuck,' cautioned an elderly monkey. But unmindful of the warning, she continued tugging at the wedged piece until it suddenly popped out. The halves of the log instantly snapped shut with the little monkey's tail and leg caught in between.

Yelling out in unbearable pain, the monkey did all she could to pull her tail and foot out. She cried in agony and then screeched in terror. The other monkeys, too, pulled and pulled with all their might, but no one could free her.

At last, the workers came back. They in turn tugged and pulled hard at the two halves and somehow managed to work her free. The workers then immediately shooed away all the monkeys.

'Uncontrolled curiosity can land you in trouble,' admonished one of the older monkeys as they were being chased away.

'Don't meddle with things that don't concern you,' advised another.

'What was the need to keep pulling at that log? We told you not to, didn't we?' cried her other monkey friends angrily.

The poor little injured monkey had no answer. She tried to limp away from the offending log as fast as she could. She had been taught a lesson she would not forget in a hurry.

Don't interfere in matters that don't concern you.

19

The Gander and the Hunter

The old gander flapped his wings in alarm. 'Oh no, is that a vine I see?' he wondered uneasily. He waddled across to the foot of the fig tree. It was a lovely old tree with long slender trunks, leafy branches and nests spread all over its thick foliage. It was home to many families of young geese.

To his dismay, the gander found that his eyes hadn't deceived him at all. It was indeed a vine.

He called out to all the other geese that lived on the tree. 'There is a vine growing at the base of this tree.'

'So what?' asked a young gosling.

'We need to cut it down now while it's supple and tender,' the gander continued.

'Why?' queried another fledgling.

'Because once it starts to grow, it will turn hard and strong, entwine the whole tree and become difficult to cut down. Anyone will be able to climb the tree and attack us,' the gander warned.

'It's only a small tender sprout,' scoffed a goose. 'It will take years to grow. Why worry about it now?'

No one was willing to heed the old gander's words. But the gander was still concerned. He screeched and squawked, flew up and down, flapped and flapped his wings so many times that another of the younger geese turned around and finally told him, 'Do shut up, you old geezer. Nothing will happen to us. No one will be able to climb the tree or kill us.'

The poor old gander retired angry and hurt. He decided he wouldn't say another word about it.

Many seasons passed. The tree aged gracefully, while the vine grew big and strong. Soon, just as the gander predicted, it entwined the entire tree right up to the crown. Now anyone could easily climb up to the top.

One fine day, a hunter passing by spotted the flock of handsome geese on the tree. 'What a nice healthy flock!' he exclaimed excitedly to himself. 'These birds will make many a good meal.' When all the geese were away, he climbed the tree with the help of the strong vine and laid a neat trap to ensnare the geese.

It was dark when the geese came home to roost. They went about their usual business and settled down in their respective places. The moment they did, the hunter's nets fell all around the tree. No matter how hard the birds struggled, there was no way out.

The geese now turned to the old gander, squawking and distressed. 'How do we get out?' they cried. 'Help us! We should have listened to you. Please think of something, or we will die.'

The old gander thought for a while. Then, nodding his wise old head, he said, 'I have a plan.'

When the hunter came the next day, every goose held its breath and played dead. The hunter saw the motionless birds and believed they were truly dead. He got angry and threw them down to the ground, one by one. They lay absolutely still, until all of them were on the ground.

To his surprise, the moment he started to climb down the vine, they rose as one and fluttered away into the skies. The vine stood firm and strong, but the geese all flew away to live another day.

'Thank you,' said the geese to the old gander, 'but for you, we would all be dead. We will never doubt or ridicule you ever again.'

Listen to the advice of your experienced elders.

20

The Mouse-girl and Her Suitor

The hawk glided high over the gushing river. Clamped in his sharp talons was his supper – a little mouse. The mouse wriggled hard as the hawk began to descend. The hawk's grip loosened, and the mouse escaped into the air.

'Please God. Help me,' prayed the little mouse as it went hurtling down. 'Don't let me die.'

God must have heard the little mouse's prayers. A sage was standing knee-deep in water with his eyes turned to the sun and his palms open. Something suddenly fell out of the sky into his upturned hands. It was the little mouse. The sage looked up and saw the hawk preparing to swoop down to pick up the mouse.

'I have to save it from the hawk,' decided the sage. He quickly got out of the river, placed the mouse onto a peepal leaf and hid it behind a bush. Unable to find the mouse, the hawk flew away, disappointed.

'Now what do I do with you?' wondered the sage, looking at the mouse. He was a venerable man with great mystic powers who could work miracles. He could even change animals into humans and humans into animals. He looked at the frightened little mouse and thought to himself, 'Why don't I change it into a human child?' He fixed his eyes on the mouse and concentrated hard, until it slowly took the form of a baby girl.

He took the baby to his wife. 'Since we don't have any children of our own, shall we adopt her as our daughter?' he asked. His wife was only too happy to agree. She had long wanted a child and joyfully welcomed the baby girl into her home.

The years passed and the little mouse-girl grew into a lovely young lady. She was both loving and kind, and her parents adored her. When the time came, the sage began to plan her wedding. He wanted the best suitor he could find for his daughter. She deserved none less than the sun god himself, he thought.

He approached the sun god and asked him if he would marry his daughter. The sun god happily agreed. He then turned to his daughter and asked, 'Will you marry the sun god, who lights up the entire world?'

'No, father,' replied the mouse-girl, 'he will burn me up. Please find me someone else.'

The sun god then suggested the cloud god. 'He is more powerful than I am. He is the only one who can block my powers.'

'No, no,' said the mouse-girl. 'He is too cold and dark. Not the cloud god, please.'

'Then why not the wind god?' proposed the cloud god himself. 'He is much stronger than I am. He is the only one who can move me around at will.'

'No, no,' said the mouse-girl again. 'Not the wind god, please. He is neither stable nor steady.'

'Then perhaps the mountain god?' offered the wind god in turn. 'He is even tougher than I am. He is the only one who is able to stop me in my path.'

'No, not the mountain god either,' said the mouse-girl. 'He is so large and immovable.'

'All right, then,' said the mountain god. 'If you won't have me, why not the mouse king? He is much more spirited than I am. He is soft and small, but he can drill holes through me anytime and go anywhere he chooses.'

The moment the mouse-girl saw the mouse king, her face lit up with joy. 'Yes, father, this is the bridegroom for me. He is soft and gentle. I can relate to him,' she sighed happily.

The learned man now realized that even if you change someone's outer self, you can't really change their true nature. A mouse will remain a mouse at heart, even if it is turned into a girl.

He promptly turned the mouse-girl back into a mouse again, and off she went with the mouse king, who was very happy to marry her.

You can't change someone's true nature.

21

The Donkey Without Brains

'No. I don't want to meet him,' said the donkey.
'You must,' insisted the fox. 'The lion has especially
asked for you.'

'Why me?' asked the donkey, refusing to move.

'He wants to make you his minister-in-chief,' the fox
replied.

The donkey laughed disbelievingly. 'Given a chance, he
will try to eat me up instead.'

'I promise he won't,' replied the fox, 'he thinks you are
smart and capable.'

'I don't believe you, and I don't trust you either,' answered the donkey. 'Don't try to flatter me with kind words.'

Now the lion that they were talking about was getting on in years. He had found himself getting weaker and weaker, with no energy to chase and kill. So he had called for the fox and said, 'I am the king of the jungle. It is your duty to look after my needs. You will bring me an animal a day as my supper. If you don't, I will eat you instead.' With no other option in sight, the fox had quickly agreed.

The clever fox knew he had to quickly do something for his own survival. He had gone out looking for a meal for the lion, and that's when he had come across this plump and well-fed donkey. 'This donkey will keep the lion well-fed for many days,' he thought. 'But I will have to cleverly lure him to the lion.' However, the suspicious donkey was having none of it.

The cunning fox was nothing if not persistent. He continued to coax and flatter the donkey, saying, 'My friend, you are wise and clever. The king of the jungle recognizes that.' At last, the donkey very reluctantly agreed and accompanied the fox to meet the lion.

The moment he saw the donkey, the lion began to lick his lips in great anticipation. Seeing the approaching lion, the donkey suddenly took fright and ran away. The hungry lion was very angry. 'If you don't catch him and bring him back, I will have *you* for supper instead,' he threatened the fox.

'You frightened him,' retorted the fox. 'I will find you another animal.'

'No,' roared the lion. 'The donkey is plump and fleshy. I want him. Bring him to me at once, or else I will have your hide.'

The wicked fox didn't want to die. He went back to the donkey and pleaded with him again. 'Please meet the lion,' he said. 'He didn't attack you when you met him the last time, did he? Why are you so afraid?'

'He came too close to me,' said the donkey.

'He may have wanted to talk to you in confidence. After all, he wants to make you his minister,' replied the fox.

'No. I don't trust him,' the donkey insisted. The fox still wouldn't give up and the donkey was eventually persuaded to meet with the lion again.

This time, the lion was craftier. He came forward slowly. He smiled charmingly and said 'hello' to the donkey before pouncing on him quickly, without giving him a chance to bolt. The poor donkey didn't know what hit him. He died instantly.

Once he had killed the donkey, the lion told the fox, 'I'm going to clean myself up. Keep an eye on the carcass. Don't let anyone touch it till I get back.'

The fox looked at the fresh meat longingly. He was hungry too. He grumbled to himself, 'I did all the hard work, and he gets to eat the juicy donkey. This is unfair!' He decided to take a bite of the donkey's head. But he ended up digging deeper and ate up its brain as well. He was sitting back and licking his whiskers in satisfaction when the lion reappeared.

The lion at once spotted the half eaten carcass. 'Who touched my supper?' he demanded.

'No one,' lied the fox, petrified.

'Then where is the brain?' the lion bellowed angrily. The fox knew he would have to use his wits once again. He thought quickly and then asked, 'What brain, sire? If the donkey had any brains would it have agreed to meet you again? The donkey has no brains.'

The silly lion believed him, and the sly fox escaped being killed.

A quick wit saves lives.

22

The Owl and the Crow

The owl plumped up his feathers and fluffed out his chest. He felt happy and proud – after all, he was going to be crowned king of the birds! 'I will be a fair and just king,' he said to himself as he waited for the coronation. 'No hunter shall dare trap any bird so long as I am here.'

The coronation was taking place because the birds had wanted to elect a new king. Their previous king had been well-respected and feared around the world, but he had no time for them. 'Who shall we choose?' the swans had asked.

'Somebody smart,' the partridges had said.

'Someone wise and kind as well,' chipped in all the cranes, the cuckoos and the nightingales.

The owl was sitting in solitary splendour, nodding his head wisely. Spotting him, the birds all chirped in unison, 'The owl, the owl – why not the owl? He will make a good king.'

And so it was done. The owl was unanimously chosen as their new king.

Now the celebrations leading up to the coronation were in full swing. The cuckoos brought in water from the holy rivers. The parrots set up the drums, and the nightingales were ready with the music. The chanting had begun.

'Where are the conches?' asked the kingfishers. 'No coronation is complete without conches blowing.'

'Lay out the feast now,' commanded the peacock, spreading his colourful tail. 'And decorate the throne.'

The koels and the doves and the swallows all set to work. They borrowed a flower here and a flower there and did up the place to look grand and beautiful.

'Now let the coronation begin,' announced the swan.

Just as the owl was about to be led to the throne, a crow happened to pass by. 'What is happening here?' he asked.

'A coronation,' the birds cried.

The crow was piqued. 'Nobody told me about it. Where are the crows? Why have you kept us out?'

'If you had been here you would have been consulted too,' the birds chorused.

'Who have you chosen?' asked the crow.

'The majestic owl,' they said.

'Why?' asked the crow.

'Because he is wise, and he looks very impressive. We think he will make a good king,' they replied.

'But you already have a great king,' cried the crow. 'His name strikes fear around the world. What better king than the great venerable eagle? How can you replace him with a half-blind owl? Do you really want such an ugly fellow as your king?'

The crow's words stopped all the birds in their tracks, and they began to feel doubtful. 'Should we call off the coronation then?' they asked each other. After much back and forth, they finally decided to meet another day to decide on their new king. And one by one they flew away, leaving the owl, his wife and the crow behind.

'What's happening?' asked the owl, who hadn't really understood what was going on. 'Why are they all leaving?'

'This nasty crow is responsible,' said his wife, who had heard the crow decry her husband. 'He called you ugly and half blind. He said you were not fit to be a king, so the birds have called off the coronation and flown away.'

'What have I ever done to you that you should do this to me? Why did you say such hurtful things about me?' the owl hooted in anger at the crow.

'I am so sorry,' said the crow, realizing his thoughtlessness. 'I spoke without thinking.'

'Well, it's too late now,' said the owl, hurt and disappointed. 'You are no longer my friend. All crows are henceforth enemies of the owl.' With that, he and his wife took off, leaving the crow rather shamefaced.

'Now why was I so tactless?' asked the crow of himself. 'What made me say all that? My reckless tongue has made me a bitter enemy. I should have kept my mouth shut.'

Unkind words make bitter enemies.

23

The Mouse and the Hermit

'Jump higher,' cried the mice. 'You can do it! Try once more,' they urged encouragingly.

Thus egged on, the head-mouse jumped again. This time, he managed to reach the bowl of food hung high on a peg. The mice waited, squealing excitedly. After all, it was their dinner he was trying to reach.

The head-mouse quickly filled his belly and threw the rest of the food down to his comrades. He rounded up as much as he could to hoard in his little hole and scampered away quickly. 'We need to get out before the hermit comes,' he warned the others.

The hermit could hear the scuffling of little feet. He knew the mice were at it again. He rushed to the kitchen, only to see his bowl empty as the thieving mice disappeared around his house.

'What do I do?' he asked himself in frustration. The hermit collected food from the households in town every day, saving some to be distributed amongst the workers of the temple where he prayed. 'No matter how high I place the food, it's gone the next day. How do I stop these mice from eating up my workers' dinner?' he wondered.

'If I get a stick and make a noise, it might frighten them away,' he decided.

So he got himself a stick and used it every night to scare the mice away. But the moment he nodded off, they would be back to empty the bowl again. He was soon exhausted from these sleepless nights and the temple workers were beginning to grow annoyed at not getting their food.

One day, a sage dropped by while the hermit was still tiredly pondering over the issue. 'What is the matter, my friend? You look tired and dispirited,' said the sage.

The hermit explained what was going on. 'As long as I am beating the bowl the food is safe, but the moment I stop, the head-mouse steals it.'

'Do you know where he stores the food?' asked the sage.

'No,' admitted the hermit.

'Well then, we need to find it,' advised the sage. 'His energy comes from that stolen food. Once we find where it is stored and destroy it, he won't have the strength to jump so high.'

The hermit took his advice and began to follow the head-mouse around. But try as he might, he couldn't find its hole.

Now the head-mouse was a clever fellow. He had overheard the men talking and knew what the hermit was up to. To prevent their plan from working, he kept changing his route every night and told all the other mice to do so too.

His plan worked perfectly … until the mice were attacked by a cat one night. Many of the mice were injured. The survivors limped home.

The next day, the hermit saw a trail of blood outside his home. 'How strange. Could this be mouse blood?' he wondered. He followed the trail, which led right up to the head-mouse's hole, where he was pleased to find the stockpiled food. He destroyed it immediately.

That night, the hermit kept some food in the bowl as usual but put some in a bag under his pillow as well to keep it safe. When the mice reappeared as usual, the head-mouse jumped high and hard but was unable to reach the bowl. He flopped back miserably on the ground again and again. 'The sage was right,' thought the hermit, going back to sleep. 'With no extra food to eat, he has no strength left to jump as high as before.'

The head-mouse, however, was not done. He decided to try stealing the food from under the hermit's head. However, the hermit woke up and hit the head-mouse hard with the stick. Injured, the head-mouse fled into its hole to lick his wounds.

The head-mouse now reflected over his sad fate. 'My food is gone, and my home has been discovered. There is no point in living here anymore,' he decided despondently. 'All my followers have left me to find another leader. I need to go and find another place to live.' And so he left.

The hermit was greatly relieved. He was glad he had followed his friend's advice. He had rid the house of mice, the food was safe, his workers were happy, and he could sleep peacefully at night.

Remove the root cause of the trouble to solve problems.

24

The Crab and the Man

The young man laughed when he saw the small little crab. 'Come on, ma,' he said, 'do you really think this little fellow is going to save me from danger?'

His mother looked at him sternly. 'You are not to go alone. It's a long journey and the path to the next town is fraught with danger. There are all sorts of animals lurking in the dense jungle. You have to take somebody with you.'

'But this tiny creature, ma?' he laughed. 'Do you seriously believe it can fight all those animals you think may attack me? A dog would be more useful. It could at least walk beside me and bark at danger.'

'No, my son. You are not to go alone. I can think of no one else but this crab to accompany you. It is a good and loyal companion. I will put it in a box, and you can carry it in your bag. You will not even know it is there.'

'Yes, that's what I am afraid of,' grinned the young man. 'The crab will be of no use to me at all.'

The little crab was extremely offended. He thought to himself, 'I may be small, but I have fought for my survival all these years. This young man thinks I am useless, but when the time comes, I will show him. His mother has been kind to me, and I won't let her down.'

The young man didn't want to displease or disobey his mother. He set out the next day, carrying a small camphor box that housed the little crab. He pushed the box deep down into his bag and soon forgot all about it.

He walked and he walked and he walked. He cut through thick foliage, swam through rivers and climbed over heavy thickets. After he had travelled a fair bit, he grew tired and decided it was time to rest. He chose a tree that reminded him of home. The tree was large and shady. It was home to many a bird and butterfly – but also home to a big cobra that lived deep down amongst its roots. The young man knew nothing of this. He settled down under the tree, placed the bag next to him and promptly fell asleep, exhausted from all that walking.

As it grew darker, the cobra emerged from its hole to find the sleeping young man. But before it could attack him, it was distracted by the smell of the camphor from the crab's box. It tried to strike at the box. As the cobra struck at it, the box fell open and the crab managed to escape.

The crab quickly realized what was happening. As the snake spread its hood again and swung from side to side, preparing to attack the sleeping boy, but the little crab pounced on the snake's neck. It dug its claws into the snake's throat and squeezed hard.

The snake began to suffocate. It tried to throw the crab off, but the crab only tightened its stranglehold. Unable to breathe, the snake struggled haplessly until it finally dropped dead.

The young man, unaware, slept through it all.

The next morning, he woke up to find the crab sitting next to him, as if guarding him, while the snake lay dead. The young man realized how wrong he had been. 'Mother was right after all,' he thought. 'Courage and determination do not belong only to the big and strong. I will never underestimate the power of a small creature again.'

Courage and bravery come in all sizes.

25

The King Frog and the Cobra

There were small frogs and there were tiny frogs. Large ones and huge ones. Some were black, many were dirty brown and others a slimy green. They all lived in a well and fought incessantly. Their croaking was so shrill, it could be heard a mile away.

The king frog was fed up. He would often shout, 'Stop your constant quarrelling! If you can't live peacefully with each other, I will throw you all out of the well.' He would then angrily hop away to his corner where he hoped to get some peace. But of course, though there was quiet for a while, the frogs would promptly go back to quarrelling again.

It soon got too much for the king frog. In sheer desperation, he leapt out of the well and onto the ground above. As he rounded the corner, the king frog spotted his old enemy – the cobra.

An idea struck him. 'How are you?' he asked the cobra concernedly.

'I am fine,' replied the surprised cobra.

'Are you eating properly?' asked the king frog with even more concern.

'Why, are you offering yourself?' asked the snake slyly.

'No, not me – but some of my relatives perhaps,' said the king frog.

'What do you mean?' asked the snake, astonished.

'Well, if I promise you a continuous supply of frogs, do you think you could come and live in my well?' the king frog asked.

'But why in heaven's name would you want me to eat your people?' asked the shocked snake.

'I am tired of their quarrels,' replied the king frog. 'I wish to get rid of them and live in peace.'

'Well, all right,' said the snake hesitantly. 'I will come and live in your well. But the well is full of water.'

'Don't worry, I'll find you a dry place,' said the king frog.

'All right then. You point out the frogs you want to get rid of, and I will eat them up one by one,' offered the snake.

'Perfect,' agreed the king frog happily and took the snake to the well and settled him on the lowermost step that had no water.

Over the next few days, the king frog began to point out his most bothersome relatives one by one. The snake did what he had to do, and there was peace all around. The snake was happy that he didn't have to go searching for food. And the king frog was happy to be getting rid of his most troublesome relatives so effortlessly.

When almost all the frogs were gone, the snake naturally asked for more.

'Well,' the king frog told him, 'your work here is done. You can go home now.'

'No,' said the snake, 'this is my home now. You will have to continue feeding me.'

'But only my immediate family is left,' said the king frog in shock.

'Well then, your family it will have to be,' said the cobra.

The king frog began to worry. 'Now what do I do?' he asked himself. 'He is going to eat me up next if I am not careful. It serves me right. I should have known he would turn against me. I should never have brought him into my home.'

The king frog needed to escape without making the snake suspicious. He hatched a plan. When only he and his wife were left, the king frog told the snake, 'Let me go out and find you some more frogs to eat.'

The snake reluctantly agreed and let him go. The frog and his wife hopped out and escaped to another well.

The cobra waited a long time before sending a nearby lizard to find out why the king frog hadn't returned. 'Tell him I won't harm him,' he said. 'He is my friend and has fed me all these months.'

'No way,' said the frog when the lizard passed on the cobra's message. 'I made the mistake of my life when I brought that snake into my home. I am not going back. An enemy is always an enemy. It can never be trusted.'

An enemy will always bite the hand that feeds him.

26

The Poor, Greedy Cat

Once upon a time in a faraway kingdom, there lived an old woman. Bent and knobbly with age, she lived alone. She decided to get herself a cat for company. She searched far and wide till she stumbled upon a thin and scrawny one. It was evident that it hadn't seen good food in a long time.

'Will you come live with me?' asked the old woman. 'I am poor and have no money. But I promise to give you half of whatever I eat.' Too weak and hungry to object, the cat followed her home, and the two began to live together.

Every day, the old lady would cook them some thin watery soup. She would pour out exactly half of the soup for the cat and eat the rest. Then she would give the cat half a piece of bread and give herself the other half. It wasn't much, but it kept them from starving.

The scrawny cat continued to live life in this way, until he encountered a stranger one day.

'What can it be?' wondered the scrawny cat. 'It looks too posh to be a tiger cub. Too fat and sleek to be a lion cub.'

'Miaaow—hello!' said the stranger to the scrawny cat. 'Don't you recognize me? I used to live here a long time ago.'

'But you look so different,' said the scrawny cat.

'Ah, that's because I am now living in the palace,' said the visiting cat. 'I have the best food to feed on.'

'But how?' asked our cat, visibly impressed.

'The king's table is usually overflowing with food, so before the guests come, I dash in and grab a piece of fish or a chicken leg. That fills me up, and I am happy.'

'But that is stealing,' said the scrawny cat.

'Yes, maybe, but a missing piece is no big deal when there is so much food about,' the other said. 'The secret is in not getting caught. There are a few other cats, and we look out for each other.'

The scrawny cat began to wonder what a chicken leg or a piece of fish would taste like. 'Will you take me with you next time you go?' he asked the fat cat.

'Sure,' said the fat cat, 'but you need to be quick when dashing in and out. If you loiter, you will be caught. Then I won't be able to save you.'

That night, the scrawny cat told the old lady about his plan. 'I believe the king's table is full of food. May I go with the fat cat and try my luck?'

'No,' said the old lady. 'That's stealing, and you will be killed if you are caught. Be happy with what you have. Don't be greedy. No amount of chicken or fish is worth your life.'

But the scrawny cat wasn't about to listen to sound advice. He was sick of the old lady's soup and bread anyway. 'It *is* worth dying for,' he decided foolishly. 'In any case, I will make sure not to get caught.'

Determined, he told his friend, 'I am coming with you.'

'Remember! Don't attract attention, don't linger,' the fat cat reminded him once more.

That night, as he watched the table groan with the most incredible food he had ever seen, our cat completely forgot his friend's advice in his wonder. He leapt swiftly through the windows and right onto the table. He quickly picked up a piece of meat and, instead of vanishing with it at once, proceeded to eat it right there. In the excitement of seeing all that food, he forgot that he was not to linger. He snatched another piece and yet another.

Unfortunately for him, a palace guard saw him. Without much ado, the guard picked him up and promptly whacked him senseless. And that was the end of our scrawny cat.

When he didn't return the next night and the night after that, his mistress knew that something had happened to him. 'If only he had listened to me, he would be alive,' she wailed.

The fat cat and his friends looked on in sorrow.

Greed doesn't pay.

27

The Jackal and the Cave

'What is this?' remarked the jackal in surprise. He was returning home after a long day when he spotted footprints near the entrance to his cave. 'These look like large paw marks. I wonder who they belong to?'

The jackal was quick-witted. Looking at the paw marks, he observed, 'They seem to be leading into the cave. But I don't see any marks leading back out, so whoever has gone into the cave is still in there. Now how do I find out who it is?'

The jackal had been living in this cave for years. It was far away from the main jungle and was well hidden by the thick leafy branches of a tree that almost covered its entire mouth. The jackal believed that no one else knew of its existence.

But unknown to the jackal, a lion had found his cave. Those paw marks belonged to the lion. It had been days since the lion had had a proper meal, so he had searched and searched for food. He had looked under trees, around bushes and chased every sound he heard, but there was nothing to be had. Not a buffalo, not a deer, nor even a little rabbit to eat. He had finally stumbled upon this large cave when looking for a place to rest his tired limbs. 'Why don't I stay here for a while?' he asked himself. 'Once its dark, I'll go out again and look for a kill.'

The Jackal and the Cave

As the lion settled down, he noticed that the cave was warm and dry and looked clean and lived in. 'Could some animal be living here?' he wondered. 'If I hide in the cave and wait till it returns, I may not even have to go out again to look for my supper.'

He made himself comfortable on a nice bed of thick hay and went off to sleep. The hours went by, and day turned to night. He suddenly woke up to a scuffling sound outside the cave and licked his lips as he waited in anticipation.

Meanwhile, as we know, the jackal had seen the paw marks. 'If it is a lion,' he thought, 'it will jump on me and kill me instantly. If it is a tiger or a leopard, I will be dead before I can react. I daren't go in till I find out who it is.' He brooded over his problem for a while and then came up with a plan.

He called out, 'Hello, cave! I'm back. How was your day?'

There was absolute silence. The lion didn't know what to do. Astonished, he wondered, 'Does any cave talk?' He decided to stay quiet.

'Why aren't you replying, dear cave?' asked the jackal. 'How was your day? Did anyone come by?' He was met with complete silence once more.

The clever jackal continued, 'Don't you remember what we had decided? If you don't reply, I will know there is danger nearby. I am not to enter the cave. If you reply, I will know it is safe to come in.'

The lion was now in a real fix. He didn't know how to react.

The jackal pretended to wait and then said, 'All right, since you aren't saying anything, you must be warning me to keep away. I will leave now.' He pretended to turn around to go back the way he came.

Just then, there came a roaring echo from within the cave, 'No, no! All is safe. You can come in.'

The jackal didn't wait to hear anything more. 'It is a lion,' he told himself and ran away as fast as his legs could carry him.

While the silly lion rued his foolishness, the jackal ran away to live another day, thanks to his presence of mind.

Quick thinking can save lives.

28

The Falcon and
the Hen

They squawked and screeched. They flew up. They
flew down. They flapped and fluttered every which
way, trying to escape the man's outstretched arm.
But alas, the coop was not big enough to save them. Some
of the hens were always caught and taken away, clucking
and protesting.

A falcon sat high on a branch of a tree, watching the scene
below. He was puzzled. 'Why do these chickens always try to
run away from their caretaker?' he wondered. 'They are given
plenty to eat. They have a nice, dry and comfortable place to
sleep in and the coop is cleaned every day. Yet, they seem so
agitated and unhappy.' He decided to ask one of them.

He flew down from his perch and hopped across to a large plump hen that was busy pecking away at her bowl of grains.

'Excuse me,' he said. 'I have been observing all of you these past days. Why is it that you protest so much and try to get away from the man who gives you food and water? Aren't you being ungrateful?'

'Ungrateful? Why, what makes you say that?' asked the hen.

'I am a wild bird,' said the falcon. 'I can go anywhere I wish, when I wish, yet I am grateful to any man who looks after me. I obey him and do whatever he tells me to. You, on the other hand, try to escape your master whenever he comes to you.'

The hen looked at the falcon most sorrowfully and said, 'Have you not noticed that every time our master comes to take some of us out, they do not return?'

'I hadn't noticed that,' said the falcon most casually. 'All I know is that you hens make such a ruckus when he comes that it wakes up the entire neighbourhood. When *my* master whistles for me, I fly to his side without a sound. I think you hens are a very ungrateful bunch of birds.'

'Well then,' replied the hen angrily. 'Before you judge us so harshly, why don't you follow our master one day and see what happens to the hens that are caught and taken away?'

'I think I will,' said the falcon huffily.

When the man came along the next time and took some hens away, the falcon followed him. To his horror, he found that the birds were being taken to be killed and cleaned. Shocked, he asked the hen, 'Is that what happens each time?'

'Yes,' nodded the hen. 'They feed us and look after us only to slaughter us. Now do you see why we try to escape the man?'

The falcon hung his head in shame and sorrow. 'Yes, I understand now,' he agreed. 'I am sorry. I should not have judged you without knowing what the truth was. I know now that everything is not always as it seems.'

Don't jump to conclusions. Things are not always how they appear.

29

The Monkeys and the Bird

They blew and they blew. Yet, it wouldn't light up. They added a twig here and a twig there. They collected more leaves. They tried to blow again. They huffed and they puffed with all their collective might. But still, the orange-red uneven balls did not burst into flames. They hunted around for more orange-red balls and excitedly added them to the heap, blowing on them again.

It was freezing amongst the mountains, and a group of monkeys was trying to light a fire. They had found some orange-red berries and foolishly mistaken them for coal embers. They were now desperately trying to get a fire going with the berries to keep themselves warm.

'Please hurry,' said a little monkey through chattering teeth. 'It is so cold, I think my fur has turned to ice.'

It was the height of winter. There were icicles all around, and the ground was as cold and hard as could be. The open mountain slope was not the best place to be in such foul weather. While some monkeys huddled together in groups and shivered, others were busy scouting for stuff to make a fire. 'Here, take these. They will come in handy,' said one monkey to another, handing him more red berries. 'They look red enough.'

'But they aren't hot, nor even warm,' said the other monkey doubtfully.

'That's because they are not,' a bird chipped in from above. Watching the monkeys' antics from his warm nest, the bird said, 'You silly monkeys, those are not coal embers. If they were, they would have burnt your hands by now. Those are red berries from the tree. They are only good to eat, not to warm.'

'Who asked you?' asked one of the monkeys. 'We don't need your advice.'

'All right,' said the bird condescendingly. 'Don't listen to me. Carry on with what you are doing. If you ask me, you will all soon die of cold.'

'Nobody asked you,' the monkeys said. 'Don't you understand? We don't want your advice. We know what we are doing.'

'No, you don't,' cried the bird, unable to keep quiet. 'Coal is black. Its embers are red. They are hot to touch and ourn your fingers. These orange-red balls that you are blowing on are just berries.'

'Stop your babbling,' said the monkeys again, more angrily this time. 'Even if you are right, we don't care. Please mind your own business.'

However, the bird still wouldn't keep quiet. 'Instead of wasting time blowing on fruit, why don't you be sensible and go look for a cave to shelter you from the cold? See how nice and warm we are in our nests!'

'Good for you,' said the monkeys. 'Now please leave us alone to do what we have to do.'

But since the bird knew he was right, he just wouldn't stop. He began to instruct the monkeys, thinking that he was being helpful. But to the monkeys, it sounded patronizing. 'There is a cave down below,' he said loudly. 'Go look for it. It will keep you warm and out of the cold. You just need to hop a little way down the slope.'

This further piece of advice only irritated the foolish monkeys more. In exasperation, one of the older monkeys jumped up and said threateningly, 'If you don't keep quiet, I will throttle you.'

But the bird continued to hold forth with more unappreciated advice. At last, the monkey, already peeved by the cold and lack of warmth, pounced on the bird and felled him with one massive stroke. The poor bird died instantly.

'What was the use of all that wisdom if he didn't know when to keep quiet?' murmured the other birds, snug in their nests.

'There is no point in spouting words of wisdom to those who do not wish to hear it. It's wiser to keep quiet,' said the old owl.

But alas, this advice came too late for the bird who didn't know when to keep quiet.

Don't give unsolicited advice.

30

The Hen With Golden Eggs

The farmer's wife was extremely angry. 'What on earth have you got there?' she asked, pointing to the hen under her husband's arm. 'Is that all you got for your bag of rice today?'

'Yes,' stammered the farmer. 'A poor man came to me and begged me for the rice. He didn't have any money. Nor did he have anything else to pay me with except this hen.'

'So you fell for his cock and bull story?' she sighed exasperatedly. 'And you are so rich that you gave up your bag of rice for a measly hen, which will be of no use to us. How could you do this to us? How do I feed our children? If only you had been sensible and exchanged it for something that would keep us from hunger, we would have been better off.'

'I am sorry,' said the farmer. 'The man was very poor. He had nothing to feed his children with, so I felt sorry for him.'

'Well then, you can keep feeling sorry for every poor fellow who spins you a story while your family slowly starves to death,' she said, stomping off. 'A hen indeed,' she muttered under her breath. 'For a whole bag of rice. What was he thinking? No wonder we are always poor. Knowing our luck, I am sure the hen will turn out barren too.'

Meanwhile, the farmer set to work and built a nice little coop for the hen. He spread some hay and scattered a few grains and locked it up for the night to keep it safe from thieving jackals and foxes. The hen clucked its way round the coop, found a comfortable little spot and promptly went off to sleep.

The farmer went back into his little hut and shared the meagre gruel and potato his wife had cooked for them. 'My wife is right,' he told himself, 'I should have bartered the bag of rice for something to eat. My children wouldn't have had to go to sleep so hungry. What do I do with this hen now?'

The next morning was bright and sunny. The farmer's wife was on her rounds to pick up some vegetables to cook when she happened to look into the coop. To her surprise she found the hen had laid an egg. It was gold in colour. Perplexed, she picked it up and took it to her husband. The farmer took a look and said excitedly, 'The hen has given us an egg of gold.'

The farmer's wife was delighted. They were able to use the egg to buy food for the whole month. Each following day saw the hen lay more golden eggs. Soon, they had a large collection of golden eggs and everything money could buy.

They prospered and lived happily, till one day, the farmer's wife began to think. She told her husband, 'This hen gives us a golden egg a day, no more, no less. I am sure it must have many more golden eggs in its stomach. What if we were to cut open the hen and take them all out in one go? That way, we won't have to wait for it every day.'

Her husband was shocked. 'Get rid of such thoughts from your mind,' he said. 'The hen has been lucky for us. If you cut it open, it will die. It is a wicked thought. I will not allow it.'

But the farmer's wife was nothing if not determined. One day, when no one was around, she caught hold of the hen and cut open its stomach … but there were no golden eggs to be found and she couldn't believe her eyes.

'Where did all those eggs come from then?' she wondered. There was no answer. The poor hen lay dead.

'If only I hadn't been so greedy,' she wailed. 'The hen would still be alive to give us more golden eggs. We will now be poor again.'

Be content with what you have.

31

The Turtle and the Swans

'No sign of any rain,' sighed the swan, looking up at the skies and shaking her slender neck. 'No,' agreed her companion. 'There is not even enough water to keep us afloat. I already find it difficult to eat or swim. Without rain, our lovely lake will dry up even faster. What do we do?'

'What are you talking about?' asked the turtle as he slowly and laboriously made his way to his two friends. 'Why are you up so late? Is anything the matter?' he asked anxiously.

'Haven't you noticed that there isn't much water left in the lake?' asked the swans. 'It's drying up. If we don't do something quickly, we will all die. Even the fish have disappeared.'

'Oh!' exclaimed the turtle. 'Well, you can't do anything about it now. The moon is up, and the hunters are out laying their traps. I suggest we turn in for the night. We can meet here tomorrow and discuss it further.'

It was dusk, and the lake was gradually taking on the colour of the night. The swans gracefully glided along home to roost amongst the lake's bushes, while the turtle shuffled back under a rock to think the matter over.

Next morning, the turtle made his way to the spot where he usually met his swan friends and was soon joined by the other two. 'I have an idea,' he said. 'Both of you can fly short distances. Why don't you scout around for another lake or pond where you can move to?'

'Good idea,' agreed the swans. 'We couldn't have come up with anything better.'

For the next few days, the two swans scouted around till they found a pond with water up to its brim. 'It's perfect,' they told the turtle. 'It looks cool, the water seems clean, and there are lots of fish and frogs swimming in it.'

'Good,' said the turtle a bit sadly. 'You go ahead and save yourselves. I will miss you sorely. You can easily fly to the new pond, but I have no way to get there.'

'No, no,' cried the swans in one voice. 'We can't leave you behind. We have been friends for years. It's unthinkable.'

They sat pondering over the issue for a while, until the turtle came up with another idea. 'If you carry a rope or a stick between the two of you, I can cling onto it until we reach the new pond. How does that sound?' he asked eagerly.

'Great idea,' cried his friends, flapping their wings. 'You will need to bite the stick while we ferry you over and across to the pond. But whatever happens, don't open your mouth or you will fall off, and we won't be able to catch you.'

The turtle agreed happily. They found a thin but sturdy stick. The turtle sank his teeth into the stick and clung on tight, while the swans carried each end. Thus settled, the three of them flew across the dried-up lake and over the fields to the new pond.

Just before they reached their new home, they were spotted by some people on the ground. 'Are our eyes deceiving us? Is that turtle actually flying? Look, look,' they cried in astonishment. Hearing all the racket below, our turtle looked down. In his excitement, he forgot that his friends had told him to keep his mouth shut. He opened his mouth to ask what the noise was all about, and the moment he did, he lost his grip and hurtled straight to the ground.

His two friends could do nothing to save him. 'If only he had remembered our advice,' they said sorrowfully, 'he would still be alive.'

Always remember to follow the advice of true friends.

32

The Crocodile, the Good Samaritan and the Fox

A wily crocodile lived on the banks of a small pond that had seen better days. He had gone without food for many days. 'I must find something to eat soon or I'll die,' he told himself. He swam up and down restlessly, hoping to surprise a kill.

Suddenly, who should come along but a strong healthy man!

'I will eat him up after I find out where he is going,' decided the crocodile. Popping out of the pond, he asked, 'Where are you going, sir?'

'I am going to a holy river a few miles from here,' replied the man.

'Is the river big?' asked the crocodile.

'Yes,' nodded the man. 'It runs the length and breadth of the country.'

The crocodile instantly decided to go along too. 'After all, there may be more food there than here,' he thought.

'Please, will you put me in your bag and take me with you?' he pleaded. 'I have no family, and I am all alone here.'

The man was a kind-hearted soul. He agreed to let the crocodile creep into the bag. Though the bag was heavy, he tied it up and lugged it all the way to the banks of the holy river. Finally, standing on the banks of the river's roaring waters, he opened the bag. 'Go along now,' said the man to the crocodile, 'here is the river.'

Instead of slipping away as the man expected, the crocodile turned around and caught the man between his large ugly teeth.

'What are you doing?' cried the man. 'Is this how you repay kindness? By eating me up? What an ungrateful creature you are.'

'Don't you know that life itself is all about turning on the person who helps you?' said the crocodile. 'I am not being ungrateful. I am only following the natural order of things.'

'How can that be?' asked the man. 'I help you, and in return you kill me? Is that fair?'

The crocodile was not prepared to listen, but the man continued pleading, to buy himself some time. 'I'll make you a deal,' he suggested. 'Let's ask three other people to decide. If they agree with what you say, I will allow you to eat me up.' The crocodile agreed.

They began by asking the big fruit tree that they were standing under. 'Oh tree, can a good deed be repaid by a wicked deed?' cried the man.

The tree thought it over and said, 'Men eat my fruit, use my leaves, share my shade and then chop me down without a second thought. That is the natural order of things. So yes, it can.'

Disappointed, the man looked around for a second person to ask. He saw an old cow sauntering by and asked her, 'Oh cow, can kindness be repaid by unkindness?'

The cow replied, 'Human beings drink my milk and use my dung, but they kill me without hesitation the moment I am useless. So yes, it can.'

The crocodile was jubilant at this reply, and the man was beginning to lose hope. A fox happened to go by just then. Desperate, the man called out, 'Mr Fox, this crocodile begged me to carry him in my bag all the way to this river. I did. Now, instead of being grateful, he wants to eat me. Is that fair? You decide.'

The fox felt sorry for the good man. He looked at the bag doubtfully. 'I don't believe you could have carried such a big crocodile in a bag as tiny as this,' he said.

'But I did,' insisted the man.

'I don't believe you,' said the fox.

'Yes, he did,' agreed the crocodile.

'You will have to show me then,' said the fox. The crocodile went back into the bag. The man quickly tied up the bag and killed the crocodile.

He gratefully thanked the fox for his help, and in return, the fox feasted on the crocodile for many days.

Good begets good; evil begets evil.

33

The Cobra, the Jackal and the Crows

The cobra waited. The moment he saw the parents leave, he stealthily slunk up the tree, got into the nest and, without wasting a minute, ate up all the newly hatched baby crows. Making sure that nobody saw him, he slithered down and went back quickly into his hole, which was the hollow of the same tree.

The mother crow returned first. She searched high and low for her babies. She flew here and she flew there. She flew up. She flew down. She flew all around the tree. Agitated, she asked the other birds, 'Do you know what has happened to my children? I was very careful this time. I left them on the highest branch and covered them so that nobody could find them.' But none of the other birds had been around to see or hear anything.

Her grief was so heart-rending that a jackal came out from a nearby hollow to enquire. 'What is the matter, Mrs Crow? Why are you crying?'

Mr Crow, who also had been away, returned just then. Sobbing, she told the two of them the story of her missing children. 'And it's not the first time,' she said, 'that this has happened. Every time my eggs hatch, they disappear within days. I'm sure the cobra that lives in our tree is eating them up, but I don't know what to do.'

The jackal was a clever fellow. 'Don't despair, Mrs Crow, we will get to the bottom of it. Just tell me the next time you lay your eggs.'

The crows agreed. Soon, a new batch of eggs was laid. The crows took them right up to the top of the tree, wove a thicker nest and camouflaged it with as many twigs and leaves they could find. When the eggs hatched, they told the jackal, 'Dear friend, our eggs are newly hatched. We have to both go out and look for food now. Please keep an eye on our babies.'

'Don't worry,' said the jackal and sent them on their way before hiding behind some bushes to lie in wait.

A little while after the couple had left, the wicked cobra came out of his hole as usual. He looked around to see if the coast was clear and stealthily attempted to make his way up.

'Aha! So you are the culprit,' said the jackal to himself. 'Now you will see how we deal with you.' And before the cobra could get to the crows' nest, the jackal made so much noise that the cobra was scared back into his hole. The jackal then stood guard till the crows returned.

'You were right, Mrs Crow. The cobra is the murderer,' he said as soon as they got home.

'But what do we do? He is dangerous and wicked. How do we tackle him?' asked the father crow.

The jackal had been pondering over this issue. 'Don't worry,' he said. 'I have an idea. What you need to do is steal some jewellery on your next trip out. Make enough noise to alert the people who own them. They must know you've taken the jewels. Then come and drop the jewels near the snake's hole.'

The crows followed the jackal's advice and flew around till they found some women bathing in a river nearby. They cawed so loudly that the women looked up, then quickly picked up the jewellery and clothes left on the banks. At once, the women alerted their menfolk who followed the crows. The crows flew straight back to their tree and dropped the stuff into the hollow. The men were still following them. When the cobra came out upon hearing all this disturbance, the men spotted him and killed him on the spot. They picked up their wives' jewellery and clothes and went home.

The crows were ecstatic. 'Thank you, dear jackal,' they cried. 'You have saved our babies. What a good friend you've turned out to be.'

A friend in need is a friend indeed.

34

The Geese and the Golden Bird

'They were very rude to me, your majesty. They told me that I was a stranger and that I had no right to swim or feed in the lake,' said the bird to the king.

The king looked hard at the bird. It was golden and looked so handsome and impressive that the king couldn't believe anybody would dare chase it away. 'Where did you say it happened?' asked the king.

'In your lake, your majesty. It is a lovely large lake, but the geese refused to let me swim there.'

'I've known the geese a long time, and they are generally friendly and undemanding. Now why would they do that?' wondered the king aloud.

'They said they paid you a golden feather as rent every few months, so it was their right to decide who is to swim in it, not yours,' the bird added slyly.

The king was immediately annoyed, just as the bird knew he would be.

'How dare they stop anyone from using my property?' he said angrily. 'How dare they usurp my right? You go ahead and swim wherever you want. I will sort them out.'

Now the lake in question was beautiful, with pristine clean waters and exotic plants. It was home to many creatures, including a flock of fine-looking geese who had made it their home for years. As the bird had mentioned, the geese paid the king a single gold feather every few weeks as a gesture of thanks. The king and the geese got on well, and so far, there had been no problems between them.

Now, however, the king was angered by the words of the golden bird and decided he needed to teach the geese a lesson. He asked his men to saddle him a horse. 'Be ready,' he said, 'to teach the geese a good lesson. They have become too arrogant for my liking.'

The geese were splashing about on the banks of the river as usual when they heard a commotion. They saw the king and his armed men making their way towards them. The head gander didn't like the look of the advancing party. 'Be ready to take off,' he told all the others. 'I think the king is in a terrible rage, and it is better to be safe than sorry. Let's get out of here fast.'

The other geese obeyed. As the king neared the lake, the entire flock lifted off, honking furiously, and flew away without even acknowledging the king. Their flight shocked the king into standing still. It suddenly struck him that his impulsive action of charging in with his men had driven away a flock that had not only lived with him for years but had also happily supplied him with many a golden feather in gratitude.

He berated himself. 'I should not have blindly believed the words of an angry stranger. Why did I not find out why they had prevented the golden bird from swimming in the lake? After all, I have known the geese far longer than I have the golden bird.'

The king rued his action. Taken in by the words of a good-looking stranger, he had acted hastily and impulsively.

Never act on an impulse.

35

The Sparrow That Humbled an Elephant

'My eggs, my nest of eggs,' cried the mother sparrow in grief. 'You have killed my babies, you horrible elephant. Couldn't you have been more careful?'

The elephant couldn't care less. He continued happily on his way, trampling everything in his path.

The elephant was both young and restless. He stomped carelessly through the forest like a lumbering giant, uprooting trees and breaking branches. Every animal in his path had run for its life, but the sparrow family that lived amongst the branches of a tree that he brought down was not so lucky. The mother sparrow's nest of eggs had been completely destroyed.

'How arrogant and wicked he is,' she remarked angrily to her husband. 'He kills our children even before they are born and is totally unrepentant. He needs to be taught a lesson.'

'How do we do that?' asked the father sparrow. 'We are so small and helpless. The elephant is big and strong, even if he is just a calf. We are lucky to have survived.'

The mother sparrow, however, was determined to have her revenge. She brooded over it for a while and decided to consult her friends. She talked to her friend, the fly, first. 'I want to avenge my babies' death,' she said. 'We need to teach that elephant a lesson. He shouldn't be allowed to get away with this!'

'It's true that we are tiny and weak compare to the elephant, but if we put our heads together, I'm sure we will find a way,' said the fly. 'Let's ask the woodpecker for help.'

They called the woodpecker and asked if he had any ideas. The woodpecker replied, 'We are all too small and puny to take on the elephant on our own. We will need more help. Let's ask our dear friend, the frog.'

So they asked the frog. The frog said, 'I have long wanted to take that elephant down. Let's sleep over it for the moment and think up a plan.'

The next morning, the frog had come up with an idea. He gathered the three around him and explained what they needed to do.

'Brilliant,' said the mother sparrow when she heard the plan. 'Let's get cracking.' And they put their plan into operation.

The fly went up to the elephant and began to buzz in his ear. This irritated the elephant so much that he started to stomp around agitatedly. The woodpecker used this opportunity to start pecking at his eyes, causing the elephant even further agony. When he heard the frog croaking, he rushed towards it, hoping to find a source of water where he could bathe his hurting eyes and stop the buzzing in his ears. But he fell straight into a deep pit that had been laid by hunters. Try as he might, he couldn't get out. He was stuck there till the hunters came and carted him off.

The mother sparrow was pleased that the frog's plan had succeeded. She told her husband, 'Where there is a will, there is a way. Even the weak and puny can take on the strong and powerful if they work together.'

Teamwork can prevail over mere strength.

36

The Cobra, the Mongoose, the Crab and the Herons

'I am tired of laying eggs,' said the lady heron to her husband tearfully, 'only to have them eaten up by that horrid cobra the moment they hatch. Let's move somewhere else.'

A crab was wandering past when he overheard her plea. He stopped to listen and saw an opportunity to get rid of the herons, his natural enemies. He went up to the couple and said, 'I am sorry, but I couldn't help overhearing your sad remark. Why don't you tell me what happened? I could help.'

They were so unhappy and desperate that they were fooled by the crab's show of concern. 'Now here's a friendly crab,' thought the herons. 'He actually wants to help instead of just gloating over our losses.'

The lady heron explained, 'For the past many months, every batch of eggs I lay disappears. However careful I am, as soon as they begin to hatch, they are eaten up by that nasty cobra that lives at the base of our tree. Unless we leave this place, I am afraid none of our young will ever survive.'

The crab thought for a while and then said, 'I have an idea. There is a mongoose who lives down the road. The snake and the mongoose are natural enemies. If we are able to lure the mongoose here to confront the snake, the mongoose will kill it in no time.'

'All right,' agreed the herons, 'but how do we get the mongoose to come here?'

'Oh, that's easy,' said the crab. 'Mongooses love fish. We will scatter some fish right up to the cobra's hole so that the mongoose will follow its trail. But we will have to entice the mongoose gradually.'

'I don't like the idea,' said the lady heron. 'It's too dangerous. There is a chance that the mongoose could attack us as well.'

'Why should it?' asked the crab. 'He won't even know you live there.'

The lady heron was still a little suspicious. 'You are a crab and a natural enemy to a heron,' she pointed out. 'Why are you helping us?'

'I am sorry for you, that's why,' retorted the crab. 'I have nothing to lose or gain in this.'

The herons believed his words and decided to follow his plan. They got some fish and began to scatter it to form a trail from the mongoose's home to the cobra's hole. The first night, they stopped at a point halfway to the cobra's hole. The mongoose was delighted to find a trail of delicious fish the next morning and followed it in no time. The next night, they trailed the fish even closer to the snake's hole. The mongoose was thrilled to find an even longer trail of food and lapped it up gladly. On the third night, the crab advised the herons to drop the fish right into the hole. Again, happy to discover yet another fresh trail, the mongoose followed it right up to the snake's home.

The cobra came out when he heard noises near his home. A fight ensued, and in a matter of minutes, the snake lay dead. Satisfied, the mongoose finished the rest of the fish and went home.

The herons were very happy. They could now have their babies in peace. They thanked the crab profusely. The next day, the lady heron laid her eggs and the couple went out happily to scout for food.

In the meanwhile, the mongoose came out of his home, expecting to see the usual trail of fish. He was now used to it, you see. He began to search for the fish hungrily, following the same path. He found no fish, but he did spot the heron's freshly laid eggs. He ate them all up and waited for the adult herons to return. 'They will be equally delicious and more filling,' he thought.

The lady heron's sad suspicions had come true. Thanks to the devious crab's advice, they had gotten rid of one enemy only to have to deal with another, more dangerous one.

Never trust a smooth-talking enemy.

37

The Two Parrots

'Q uick, get your bow and arrow,' screeched the parrot loudly. 'Shoot the man. Shoot the man fast!'

The king was taken aback. He had stopped by the hunter's lodge to water his horses and feed his men before embarking on a long ride through the forest.

'Don't let him get away,' screamed the parrot again. 'Kill him!'

The parrot's loud racket annoyed the king immensely. 'I have never seen such a rude and unpleasant bird in all my life,' he thought. 'I don't think I want to meet the hunter now. He could be equally disagreeable.' The king turned to his men and said, 'Let's not stop here. We will go further afield and look for food and shelter someplace else.'

The Two Parrots

As they rode on again, many miles down the road, the king spotted a spartan but beautiful ashram. 'This seems a good place to rest awhile,' he said. 'Let us find out if the sage here can give us something to eat and drink.' They stopped to speak to someone but could find no one about. Instead, the king was surprised to see the same parrot there once more.

'How can that be?' he asked himself. 'We just saw this rude parrot miles away from here!' Annoyed, he told his men, 'Let's go away. I don't wish to be spoken to so rudely again.'

As the king turned to go, the parrot called out sweetly, 'Welcome to our humble home. My master will get you and your men something to eat and drink.'

This stopped the king in his tracks. Puzzled, he turned around and asked the parrot, 'Weren't you at that hunter's lodge a few miles away from here just now?'

'No, sir, you must be mistaken. I live in this ashram and rarely go anywhere,' replied the parrot.

The king did not think he was mistaken. 'You are identical to the parrot I just saw,' he said, perplexed. 'Only your behaviour has changed drastically. But how could you have flown here so fast?'

The king was right. The parrots did look identical. From the little red tufts on their heads to their green and red feathers, there was absolutely no difference between the two.

The parrot at the ashram was startled. For a moment, he looked almost sad. He wondered to himself, 'Could the king have met my twin? A hunter did steal my brother a long time

145

ago. Maybe this means he is still alive!' He asked the king, 'May I tell you my story, sir?'

The baffled king nodded.

The parrot began, 'We were once two brothers happily chirping away in a nest, when a hunter came by while our mother was away looking for food. He climbed up our tree stealthily and managed to put us both into a bag. But as he was climbing down, I got thrown out and fell behind a bush. The hunter searched for me but gave up and left in a hurry with my poor brother in his bag. Soon after, a sage came along and found me lying on the ground. He rescued me and I've been living here at the ashram with him since then.'

Just as the parrot finished his story, the sage stepped out. He was an old and venerable man. 'Come in, sir,' he said gently, almost in the same manner as the parrot. 'Welcome. Please make yourself comfortable. What can I get you to drink?'

The king was most mystified. 'The company you keep matters,' he said to himself, reflecting on what he had just seen and heard. 'This parrot parrots what the sage says, while the other one rudely and harshly screeches, probably imitating what he has heard his master, the hunter, say. How you are trained or brought up is important and so is the company you keep.'

The king thanked the sage, saying, 'I have learnt a valuable lesson today. Politeness begets politeness. Rudeness begets rudeness.'

Other people can influence one's behaviour and nature.

38

The Deer, the Crow, the Mouse and the Tortoise

The deer struggled hard. 'If I try to bite or push I might be able to tear through the net,' he told himself. He tried to cut the net with his teeth. He thrust his legs and head hard and shoved them against its strings. But nothing worked. The hunter's net held firm and strong. The deer began to look panic-stricken.

'Why did I wander so far away from my friends?' he asked himself. 'I wonder where the mouse, the crow and the tortoise are. Will they realize I am missing and look for me?'

The Deer, the Crow, the Mouse and the Tortoise

His friends at that moment were gathered at the usual spot where they met every single day. They waited for the deer to join them and began to grow concerned when he didn't appear.

'Do you think he is in trouble?' asked the tortoise.

'Should I fly around and look for him?' asked the crow.

His friends agreed that it was a good idea, and he took off to search for the deer. As he flew around cawing, he heard a faint bleat. He flew towards the sound and found his friend all trussed up and tied in a hunter's net.

'I am so happy to see you,' cried the deer joyfully.

'We were beginning to wonder what happened to you. The others sent me to look for you,' the crow said.

'I need to get out of this net before the hunter comes,' said the deer.

'Not to worry,' said the crow. 'I will fly back and get the other two. The mouse will nibble through the net in no time.'

The crow flew back to collect the others. The tortoise decided to make his own way there, so the crow carried the mouse on his back. The mouse got to work quickly and freed the deer. The minute the deer was free, they took to their heels.

In the meanwhile, the tortoise reached the scene, huffing and puffing. While he was trying to catch his breath, the hunter arrived on the scene. He saw the net and was enraged. 'How did the deer escape?' he asked himself. He turned around to check and spotted the poor breathless tortoise. 'Ah well,' he said, 'I will make do with tortoise meat tonight instead of deer,' and bundled up the tortoise to take with him.

The deer, the mouse and the crow were waiting for the tortoise to catch up. When he didn't arrive, they went back to look for him and saw him being carried in a bag by the hunter. They were determined to save their friend, and the deer quickly came up with a plan.

They put the plan into operation, and it worked out exactly as the deer had intended. The deer first planted itself on the hunter's path. When the hunter saw the deer, he promptly dropped the tortoise and the bag and took after it. 'I will not let it escape this time,' he told himself.

But of course, he was no match for the beautiful runner. He lost the deer halfway through and turned back in disappointment … only to find his bag in shreds and the tortoise gone! The mouse had nibbled through the bag and set the tortoise free.

Scratching his head in disbelief, the hunter murmured to himself, 'They have escaped twice in one evening. I wonder how they did it!'

He wasn't to know that it was teamwork that had done it.

Good friends are a blessing.

39

The Lion, the Bull and the Jackals

The bellows were loud and clear. First the sound rang out once, then twice. The third time, it reverberated through the forest and all the animals ran for cover.

The lion heard the bellows too. He was convinced it came from an alien creature. 'Where is it coming from?' he wondered as he quickly took to his cave. 'It sounds so strong and terrible.'

His two ministers, the jackals, came looking for him. 'Sir, did you hear the bellow? What do you think it could be?' they asked.

'I don't know,' said the lion. 'It sounded overpowering.'

'Let's go find out,' said the jackals to each other.

The Lion, the Bull and the Jackals

They went in the direction of the sound. They searched and they searched, but there were no creatures to be seen other than a very ordinary looking bull grazing benignly amidst the grass. They were about to turn back when the bull saw them. He let out such a bellow that the two jackals froze. Then they fell about laughing.

'So this is the monster,' they said in relief. 'A common bull has frightened our king and all the animals in the jungle.'

Now the two jackals were sly and cunning. They loved to cause mischief. They quickly went up to the bull and said, 'Our king heard your bellows and is very angry. We suggest you come and make your peace with him, otherwise you are going to be sorry.'

But the bull had no problem with that. 'After all, he is the king of the jungle,' he told himself and said to the jackals, 'I am sorry my bellows annoyed the lion. I would be happy to apologize to him.'

The jackals then hastened to the lion. 'It is a bull, your majesty,' they laughed. 'An ordinary common bull.' Then the jackals began to lie to the lion as well. 'He says god has given him the right to roam free in the jungle,' they said, 'but we told him you were the king of the jungle and he needs to pay obeisance to you.' As they expected, the lion was flattered.

But to the jackals' dismay, when the bull was brought to meet the lion, the two took to each other at once and were soon exchanging life stories. 'I was left to die by my master, but I managed to survive and have been living here ever since,' said the bull.

The lion was sympathetic. The bull turned out to be kind and wise. They became such good friends that they began to spend most of their time together. It was a common sight to see them companionably roam the length and breadth of the forest together.

The two jackals didn't quite like this turn of affairs. They began to burn with jealousy. 'How can the lion ignore us and spend so much time with the bull?' they murmured to each other. 'We are his ministers, after all.'

They hatched a plan to break up their friendship. First, they approached the lion and told him, 'You consider the bull to be such a good friend, but he is planning to overthrow you and become king!'

'I don't believe you,' said the lion.

'It's true. When you see him next, watch how he holds himself. He plans to attack you,' insisted the jackals.

The jackals continued their wicked plan. Next, they went to the bull and said, 'The king is planning to kill you and eat you up. His appearance of friendship is all a show. You should be on guard.'

'I don't believe you,' said the bull.

'Well, see for yourself,' said the jackal, leading him to face the lion.

The moment the lion saw the bull, he recalled the jackals' words and stood ready to attack. Seeing this, the bull also took guard immediately. The lion mistook the bull's reaction and thought he was going to be attacked. He lunged forward and attacked the bull first. A massive battle followed, and in the end, the bull lay dead.

If only both the animals had verified the truth before believing the jackals.

Now the lion had lost a good friend due to the traitorous advice of some jealous jackals and the innocent bull had lost his life.

Never blindly believe others.

40

The Rabbit and the Elephants

'Don't despair. If we go a little further, I am sure we will find water,' the leader of the elephants urged.

The elephants listlessly ambled along. It was hot and dry, and they were exhausted. It had been a long trek in search of water, and they were no nearer finding any lake. As they moved forward step by step, they trampled upon yards and yards of rabbit burrows and unknowingly destroyed many little animals' homes. Not that they cared. They were too hot, bothered and thirsty to know what they were doing.

Luckily, just as their leader had predicted, they soon reached a lovely large lake. They fell upon it with great joy.

Trumpeting loudly and waving their trunks, they happily cooled off and playfully splashed each other in sheer joy.

A group of rabbits looked on at this in dismay. The rabbit king was thinking hard. He was petrified by the arrival of the meandering tribe of elephants. 'Now that they have found water, the elephants are bound to make this their home,' he said. 'At the very least, they will keep coming back to this lake. Our burrows will be destroyed, and we will have no more peace here.'

'Yes, they are a threat to our peaceful life here,' agreed the others, equally worried. 'We have to get rid of them somehow, or we will have to move!'

The rabbits called for a meeting to discuss their concerns. 'I have an idea,' offered one bold little rabbit. 'If you allow me, we can trick the elephant into believing that the lake god does not like them using his lake.'

'How will you do that?' asked the rabbit king. 'There is no lake god.'

'Leave it to me, sir,' said the little fellow confidently.

The next day, the rabbit went up to the elephant leader and said, 'Welcome, oh king, to our little kingdom. We have been living here for years. I just thought I should warn you that the moon god lives in the lake. Unfortunately, he is a little annoyed with you elephants at the moment.'

'Why?' asked the elephant leader, puzzled. 'We haven't done anything to annoy anyone. I didn't even know the lake had a god living there.'

'The moon god lives inside the lake,' explained the rabbit. 'He doesn't always come out … except when he is annoyed.'

'Why should he be annoyed with us?' the elephant king repeated.

'Oh, that's because he doesn't like anyone drinking from the lake, let alone bathing in it,' said the rabbit respectfully, 'and you elephants have been doing both.'

'I still haven't seen any god,' said the elephant king disbelievingly.

'I will introduce you to him tonight,' replied the rabbit promptly.

As promised, the little rabbit escorted the elephant king to the lake that night. Then with great ceremony, just before moonrise, he announced, 'We have come to pay our respects, dear moon god. I have brought the elephant king.' The moon rose up in the sky as if it had heard the rabbit's call, and its reflection appeared in all its splendour on the surface of the lake.

It looked so grand that the elephant king was completely fooled. He immediately fell upon his knees. 'Please don't be annoyed,' he said humbly. 'We will not use this lake hereafter. We will look for another lake.' All the rabbits watched as he herded his flock together and strode away.

The rabbits patted the little one on its back.

'Sometimes a little trickery is required to save lives,' said an elderly rabbit as they all went back into their burrows knowing that the rabbit had kept them safe.

A little deception is all right if it saves lives.

41

The Crow That
Defeated the Owls

The cry was faint and weak. 'Please, help me. Somebody, please help me.'

'All the crows seem to have fled their home. Who could this be?' wondered one of the owls. He went to check and found a wounded crow lying on the ground.

Soon, he was joined by other owls. 'Hello. What happened to you?' they cried.

'My king and his courtiers did this to me,' said the crow in a feeble voice. 'I told them to make peace with you, and they got enraged and tried to kill me. Now I want revenge. Take me to the owl king, and I will tell you where they've gone.'

'Don't listen to him,' said a senior owl. 'Kill him immediately. He is the enemy.'

'No, no,' said the others, 'we don't kill the hurt and wounded, even if it is an enemy.'

'Then let the king decide,' they said. So off they went to the owl king.

The owls all lived in a cave. As you know, owls can only see at night, so they slept during the day. The crows, on the other hand, slept only at night. Now the owls and the crows were bitter enemies. Every night the owls, with their sharp night vision, waited for a chance to attack and kill the sleepy crows. The crows were being gradually eliminated, and the crow king didn't know what to do.

The crows believed the owls were planning another attack again that night. Desperate, the crow king and all his subjects flew away to hide in a mountain nearby. Thus, when the owls reached the banyan tree, they found only this one bleeding wounded crow.

The owls brought their king to look at the injured crow. The wounded crow continued to sob, 'I have been left to die by the crow king. I promise you, I have no enmity towards you. Please don't kill me. Let me stay.'

The owl king was in a fix. He asked his ministers, 'What do we do? Even though he is wounded, he is still the enemy.'

The ministers couldn't agree on a decision. Three out of the five ministers insisted, 'We shouldn't kill someone who needs our help.'

His other two ministers said, 'Sir, an enemy is an enemy. Don't trust him. Kill him. He could be a spy.'

The owl king thought for a while and finally decided that since the crow was willing to tell them where the other crows were hiding, he should be spared. The crow was allowed to live with the owls. He chose to make his home near the entrance of the cave.

Soon, on the pretext of building himself a nest, he began to pile the entrance with all the twigs and straw he could muster. When all the owls were asleep, he stealthily flew to where the rest of the crows had hidden themselves. He told the crow king, 'I have managed to fool the owls. All is ready, your highness.'

The owls were not to know that the wounded act had been a ruse to set them up. Before the crow king had taken his subjects to the mountains, he had held a war council to decide how to deal with the murderous owls.

His ministers all had different opinions. While one of his ministers said, 'Make peace,' another said, 'Fight.' The third said, 'Wait and then strike,' while the fourth said, 'Attack with help.' The fifth minster said, 'Ask outside allies to come to our aid.' But the minister most experienced and well-versed in warfare said, 'Use spies to fool them. Then plan a strike. If you agree, I will fool the crows by pretending to be a wounded crow, spy on them and set the stage for you to retaliate.'

The crow king had agreed, and they had put the plan in action.

Now, their plan was finally almost complete. At sunrise, when the owls couldn't see, the crows flew in together and set the twigs at the entrance on fire. Every owl in the cave perished. The only ones to survive were those that had left the cave earlier because they hadn't believed the crow's story.

The crows' strategy had allowed them to get their revenge on the owls.

Plan your strategy well.

Conclusion

This is the Panchatantra.

T hus did Vishnu Sharma fulfil his promise to the great King Amar Shakti of Mahilaropya. Within six months, these stories taught Bahu Shakti, Ugra Shakti and Anantha Shakti many lessons:

Why one should not be too greedy

Why one should be content with what one has

Why one should not be arrogant or proud

Why one should not pretend to be what one is not

Why the company one keeps matters

Why one should not interfere in other people's matters

Why one should have good friends

Why it is important to keep those friends

Why teamwork pays

Why there is strength in unity

Why one must be wary of an enemy turned friend

Why one shouldn't blindly believe others

Why quick-wittedness is a great asset
Why one shouldn't jump to hasty conclusions
Why one should think well before one acts
Why one should plan wisely
Why one shouldn't forget one's origins
Why East or West, Home is the best
Why one should get to the root of any problem
Why trickery can sometimes save lives

These ideas are as relevant today as they were so many centuries ago, which is one reason why the Panchatantra has endured so long and will continue to endure for all time.

All the elephants, the jackals, the crabs, the cranes and the geese, not to forget the snakes, the monkeys, the ants, the fish and the frogs; or the deer, the crows, the owls, the lions and the rabbits – hope you've enjoyed your journey into their animal kingdom.

Acknowledgements

These stories are found in various forms as books, audios and internet/YouTube videos. For purposes of this book, the translated works of Arthur William Ryder and G.L. Chandiramani, Santhini Govindan's 71 *Golden Tales of Panchatantra* and http://www.talesofpanchatantra. com have been points of reference.

Sreelata Menon

With many children's books to
her credit, author and freelance
writer Sreelata Menon writes about
anything and everything. She
especially enjoys capturing children's
imagination with India's rich literary
legacy and its many fascinating
tales. She believes that if children are
able to relate to these stories, it will inspire and
encourage them to have aspirations of their own.

Megha Punater

Megha Punater is a freelance graphic
designer and illustrator based in
Mumbai and Pune. She has illustrated
children's books, designed books and
covers for various publishing houses
and designed brand identities for
established businesses, both in India
and abroad. She also designs textile
patterns for well-known fashion brands. When not
at her desk, Megha enjoys reading, gardening,
travelling, painting and creating mini handmade
illustrated books. Megha is a graduate of Sir J.J.
School of Art and the National Institute of Design.

The Roots of India series will bring children closer to their roots through stories that will introduce them to the India of the past, the present and the future — its mythology, its history, its geography, its people, its cities, its food and everything that constitutes the rich cultural diversity of India.

The first boxset contains a collection of some of India's greatest stories ranging from tales from the *Panchatantra* and stories of the *Mahabharata* to India's many *festivals* and its *ancient learned men and women*.

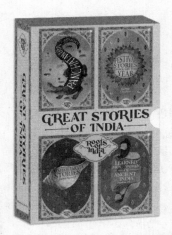